CLARA WU

AND THE

RESCUE

BY VINCENT YEE

DEDICATION

Dedicated to all the Asian Americans and our allies, who are doing everything they can to fight anti-Asian hate that has affected our communities.

CHAPTERS

ONE

The sounds of metal lockers opening and closing, the shuffling of shoes on linoleum floors, and excited teenage chatter echoed through the hall. Clara rummaged through her knapsack at the end of the day that Thursday. She pulled out a textbook and placed it into her locker. When she swung the locker door shut, Melissa Chin was staring back at her with a big grin.

Clara pulled back, startled, and quickly smiled back. She playfully tapped Melissa's right shoulder for startling her. Melissa laughed behind her cute glasses as her thick, black, shoulder-length hair framed her face.

"Don't do that!" said Clara teasingly.

"Scared ya, didn't I?" asked Melissa. "Want to get *boba?*"

Clara's eyes lit up as she adjusted her Azen bamboo hair accessory and slung her knapsack over her shoulder. "Definitely! Let's go!"

Soon they were joined by another girl, Grace Sohn, a cute Korean American with bouncy above-the-shoulder-length hair. She snuck in behind Clara as Melissa hung back to chat with her.

"Clara! What flavor *boba* are you getting?" asked Grace from behind.

Clara glanced back before looking ahead as she pondered her decision. "Earl Grey Milk Tea with three jellies," said Clara whimsically.

"So fancy! I'm going to get that too!" said Grace with a smile.

Clara looked up and sighed as her eyes rolled playfully at Hong Chen and his girlfriend Phuong Hunyh. He was leaning in toward her, his left palm pressed up against the locker by her cheek as she leaned back against the locker, smiling up at him. They were annoyingly and adorably inseparable. Hong was tall and slender, wearing a black bomber jacket and navy jeans and a faded hairstyle. Phuong looked adorable in her oversized sweater that slipped off her shoulder slightly along with blue jeans.

"Hey!" said Clara as she caught both love birds' attention. With their turned heads, they smiled. "We're gonna get *boba*, wanna come?"

Hong looked down at Phuong, who looked up while nodding with a smile. "Sure thing, Clara!" said Hong as he pushed Phuong's locker door shut and the couple fell in behind Melissa and Grace.

Soon Clara and her friends exited the front doors and bounded down the steps. Hong whipped out a pair of sunglasses and put them on as Grace did the same. As they landed on the paved path leading down to the sidewalk, Clara saw the school bully, Clarissa, who was walking up the path with her equally mean friends in tow. She furrowed her brow at Clara.

Clara turned away and walked by nonchalantly just as Clarissa uttered, "Ching chong!"

Clara shot her a look, but before she could react, a teenaged Black couple walked in between them. The teenaged Black boy, with his left arm over his girlfriend, looked at Clarissa with a smile, "Yes, we know you're stupid, Clarissa!"

Laughter erupted all around as the Black girl looked at Clara, tipped her sunglasses down, and smiled.

Clara smiled back, but she could see Clarissa's seething face staring back at her. She turned away and continued walking down the path.

Suddenly, Clara winced in pain, abruptly jerked backwards by Clarissa who pulled hard on her ponytail. "You chink!" hollered Clarissa.

Clara dropped her knapsack and gripped her hair with her left hand just above where Clarissa's hand was clutching it, regaining her balance. Instinctively, she pivoted until she was face-to-face with Clarissa, whose left fist was clenched.

Clara quickly switched her grip, scooted under Clarissa's right arm, and struck Clarissa's elbow hard and fast with her left forearm. Clarissa grunted in pain and released Clara's ponytail.

Finally separated from Clarissa, Clara assumed a fighting stance and focused on Clarissa's angry eyes as she lunged at Clara, letting out some battle cry.

Clara sidestepped Clarissa's lunge, her attempted punch and pivoted again. Clarissa lunged again, but Clara easily sidestepped her. As Clarissa flew past, Clara landed a sidekick high on Clarissa's back, sending her flat on her face.

The other students erupted in laughter as Clarissa's two friends rushed to her side. Clara stood tall and relaxed her stance as Clarissa turned over, revealing a bloodied nose.

"No more!" said Clara firmly as she pointed her finger at the defeated Clarissa.

Melissa rushed up in astonishment as she held out Clara's knapsack. Clara paused for a moment before looking at Melissa and smiling. "Thanks. Let's get that *boba*."

As Clarissa was helped up by her two friends, Clara spun away with her friends following as nothing was going to stop her from getting her earl grey milk tea with three jellies.

TWO

Clara ambled up the stairs to her apartment. After jostling with the keys, the door opened to reveal her mother's stern eyes. Clara felt her heart sink as she entered.

"Mom?" asked Clara sheepishly as her mother stepped in suddenly and slammed the door shut behind Clara. She cowered a bit as her mother pulled back with her eyes beaming.

"Don't mom me!" scolded her mother. "Were you in a fight at school earlier?"

Clara looked side-to-side when her mom stammered again.

"Don't look at the floor! Answer me!" her mother demanded.

"I was defending myself. The school bully…"

"I don't care who started it!"

"But what should I have done? Let her beat me up?"

"You shouldn't be in any fights, period!" said her mother as her voice reached a crescendo.

Clara fell silent as a mix of shame, frustration, and anger swirled up within the pit of her stomach.

"Your father and I will need to go to your school tomorrow and talk to the principal and hope that she won't suspend you. Or worse yet, expel you!" scolded her mother.

Clara's head was downcast as she tepidly held onto the top strap of her knapsack.

"Go to your room," her mother said sternly.

"But Mom…" protested Clara as she looked up with anguished eyes.

"Now!" ordered her mother which she followed up with, *quickly* in Cantonese, "*Fai-dee-ah!*".

Clara slipped out of her shoes with a feeling of resignation. She stomped down the hall toward her room in quiet resentment.

* * *

The next day, Clara sat in a wooden chair in between her parents. Her mother was dressed in black slacks with a light blue sweater and black pumps. Her father was wearing a navy-blue suit, a crisp white dress shirt with a fancy tie, and brown dress shoes.

The high school's principal had just welcomed them in as she sat down. Ms. Dunley was a white woman in her late forties, who was dressed nicely as well. Her strawberry-blondish hair was pulled back into a tight bun, as she wore a textured wool ivory skirt suit outfit.

"Mr. and Mrs. Wu, thank you for coming in today and I regret that we have to meet under these unfortunate circumstances," said Ms. Dunley warmly but without enthusiasm.

Clara's parents were silent as they nodded at Ms. Dunley. Clara stared down at her feet.

"Well, no reason to waste any more time. What your daughter did yesterday to poor Clarissa was wrong, and as you know, we don't condone violence of any sort here at our prestigious high school."

"Ahem," said Mrs. Wu as she caught Ms. Dunley's attention. "What exactly did my daughter do wrong?"

Ms. Dunley looked surprised by Mrs. Wu's question as she answered, "Well, Clara's unprovoked violent attack toward Clarissa of course."

"By whose account?" asked Mrs. Wu.

Ms. Dunley paused and gave an ungrateful look toward Mrs. Wu. She straightened up, twisted her head from side-to-side before resetting her authoritative look toward Mrs. Wu and said, "Well, from Clarissa of course."

Clara caught her father shifting in his seat as he crossed his right leg over his left. He brought up his right hand under his chin as he rested his elbow on the armrest without taking his gaze off Ms. Dunley.

Clara's eyes shifted to her mother, who opened her purse and took out her large-screen phone. Her mother calmly unlocked her phone and turned it toward Ms. Dunley.

"Ms. Dunley," said Mrs. Wu calmly. "I would like you to watch this video with me. It was sent to me by one of Clara's friends' parents, who just happened to be filming. Let's watch."

Clara's eyes widened as she saw her mother lean in with the phone. She then looked up at her father, who gave Clara a look, smirked, and motioned with his finger for her to watch. Clara turned back to her mother.

"You see here, my daughter is just passing by when this Clarissa said, "ching chong," mocking my daughter for being Chinese. Let me replay that again. There, you heard Clarissa say "ching chong," a clearly racist term. Here you can see my daughter did the right thing, took the high road, and walked away. But after the nice young Black couple walked by, Clarissa came from behind and violently yanked my daughter's hair. Here, let me replay that again. And again, my daughter did the only thing she could do: She defended herself. As you can see here, after she broke Clarissa's hold, my daughter is only defending herself. Clarissa lunged at my daughter, not once, but twice, so my daughter kicked her to the ground to end this, how did you call it, violent attack?"

Ms. Dunley pulled back, cleared her throat as Mrs. Wu settled back into her chair.

"Well, despite what I saw, your daughter should not have kicked Clarissa in the back and sent her to the ground, thus bloodying her nose."

"Are you kidding me?" interjected Mrs. Wu.

"Mrs. Wu, there is no need to raise…" said Ms. Dunley in a condescending tone before Mr. Wu interrupted her.

"Ms. Dunley," said Mr. Wu firmly as Ms. Dunley turned to him.

"Ms. Dunley," said Mr. Wu once more. "Do you know what I do for a living?"

There was a moment of silence when Ms. Dunley said snidely, "Something in Chinatown?"

Mr. Wu's expression turned incredulous as he straightened up in his chair and looked sternly as Ms. Dunley.

"I would be proud to work in Chinatown," said Mr. Wu. "But I do not. However, I do serve the great state of New York as an Assistant District Attorney."

There was silence in the office as Ms. Dunley suddenly shifted in her seat.

"As you can imagine, I have seen my fair share of criminal cases. And let me tell you, my wife and I have every right to file assault and battery charges against Clarissa."

"I don't think we need to go that far..." beseeched Ms. Dunley.

"I didn't finish," said Mr. Wu firmly. "From what I just witnessed, I saw a principal who just tried to sweep under the rug a violent White student committing what a court may consider a hate crime against my daughter. So from here on, you will not punish our daughter, and you will hold Clarissa responsible for her actions. Do I make myself clear?"

Ms. Dunley looked shaken as she looked down at her desk for a moment and then looked up with a forced smile.

"Mr. and Mrs. Wu, in light of this video, I believe there was a misunderstanding here. I see nothing here that would find Clara at fault. I think we can dispense with this matter," said Ms. Dunley calmly.

"What about Clarissa?" asked Mrs. Wu.

"Right. Clarissa. I will have a talk with her and her parents..." said Ms. Dunley.

"More than just a talk. She assaulted and used a racial slur against my daughter. I think a suspension will send a clear message. Don't you think?" asked Mrs. Wu.

Ms. Dunley looked down and cleared her throat once again.

"It would look very bad for the school to be under a lawsuit for condoning racism and violence," said Mr. Wu calmly.

Ms. Dunley looked up with her eyes widened, "Yes, suitable punishment will be acted on Clarissa to hold her accountable."

"Good. I trust that you will let us know when that punishment is doled out," said Mr. Wu.

"Yes," said Ms. Dunley. "Certainly."

Clara's mother then uttered a light cough that caught Clara's attention.

Ms. Dunley looked in Mrs. Wu's direction and feigned a smile. "Yes?"

"Are you going to apologize to my daughter?" asked her mother.

Ms. Dunley then turned toward Clara with an awkward smile.

"Clara, I want to apologize for thinking you were the aggressor," said Ms. Dunley.

"Thank you," said Clara.

"We'll be leaving now," said Mr. Wu. "But I expect an update from you before the end of today."

"Yes, of course," said Ms. Dunley.

Mr. Wu gave Ms. Dunley a stern look, then looked at his wife who nodded before she gestured to Clara to get up. Clara promptly got up and looked at Ms. Dunley and said, "Thank you, Ms. Dunley."

Ms. Dunley feigned a smile as she waved nervously.

As Clara and her parents exited the office, they walked through the administration area and then into the hallway.

"Mom! Baba! That was so cool!" exclaimed Clara as she turned to face her parents.

Her parents looked and smiled at each other before turning back to their smiling daughter.

"Clara," said her mother reassuringly. "I'm sorry I didn't want to listen to you yesterday, but I was just so scared hearing that you were in a fight, I was worried. Can you forgive me?"

Clara rushed in and hugged her mother around the waist and Mrs. Wu smiled, "Of course, Mom."

As Clara pulled back her mother asked, "By the way, when did you learn to fight?"

Clara suddenly felt caught off guard and uttered the only answer she could, "YouTube?"

"YouTube," said her father sardonically as he looked at his wife. "Kids these days, they can learn anything from the Web. Look Clara, I'm glad you can defend yourself, but you have to be very careful. There are some really bad people out there. I mean who do you think you are? Some kind of empress warrior?"

Clara suddenly felt awkwardly stupefied as she looked at each of her parents.

"Well, considering that so many people saw what you did to Clarissa, no one will bother you from now on," said her mother.

"You're probably right," said her father as he looked at her daughter. "Do we need to call you Empress Warrior Wu now?"

Clara's face crumbled as she took a step back as a huge yearning to get out suddenly filled her very being as she uttered, "Uh…"

"Clara, your mother and I are going to get on with our day now, so you get on with yours, okay?" said her father.

Clara saw her moment to escape as she nodded her head nervously as she felt her heart racing.

"Bye now, my little empress warrior Wu," said her father teasingly.

Clara's eyes bulged as she let out, "Okay! I gotta go!"

As Clara bolted away, her mother grabbed onto her grinning husband as she whispered, "Don't encourage her."

"YouTube," chuckled her father as he watched Clara dash around the corner. "You know, I used to do Kung Fu too!"

Clara's father quickly let out a straight punch with his right hand and held it out, reminiscing the days when he used to go to Kung Fu classes before he entered college.

His wife quickly patted down his arm and chided him teasingly, "Stop that. This is a high school. Do you think it's going to turn into the badlands or something?"

THREE

Clara gracefully pushed her right palm forward as her left arm pushed backwards while she moved into a forward stance. She paused her form in the middle of the bedroom and smiled as she conjured the *wall* Qi element by tracing it out and whispering, *"teng-bing."* The beautiful bluish Chinese character glowed at her fingertips, and her eyes fixated on it. Its soft radiance reflected in her brown almond eyes and she smiled.

In a fraction of a breath, she flicked it away and rose up onto her right leg, while drawing her left leg inward with a bent knee, moving her arms delicately around her in an arc as she whispered in Cantonese, *"tei-hum."* As she balanced on one leg, she glanced upward to see the bluish Chinese character for *sinkhole* in her right hand. She smiled and thought how awesome she must look in her pose.

Even cooler if she had on her Azen battle armor, she thought to herself.

Deftly, she launched into a jumping front kick as her right instep snapped into her clasped hands, snuffing out the bluish Qi element. She landed with a slight thud and assumed another elegant fighting stance. Another smile crept across her face as she stood up straight, brought her palms face down at her chest with her elbows out, exhaled slightly while pushing her hands down to her sides.

She bowed and whispered, "For Azen."

With her awakened Qi flowing through her body, infused by the experience of all the Panda Warriors past, she found that she didn't need to warm up. Every muscle in her body was at the ready. She knew that she and her fellow warriors were more than just normal martial artists. They were Azen warriors.

She could enter any and all Kung Fu tournaments and probably win them all. With that, she could probably star in some *Wuxia* movie, where she could practice her Mandarin even more. But she brushed away the whimsical thought. It wouldn't be fair.

Clara turned her gaze toward her stuffed panda, Bo Bo.

"How did I do?" asked Clara as she turned fully toward Bo Bo. That's when she saw her stuffed panda's eyes glow. Clara quickly turned toward her desk and saw that her Portal Book was glowing.

She strode over to her desk, looked down, and saw the Chinese character for *return* glowing on the page.

"Really? Mom's making *char-siu wonton mein* tonight!" lamented Clara as she thought about the tempting roasted pork wonton egg noodle dish.

Her momentary disappointment vanished as she quickly changed out of her workout clothes and into a pair of jeans, an athletic top, a zip-up activewear jacket, and clean white socks. She adjusted her ponytail and pulled it taut through her bamboo hair accessory. She settled into her chair as the glow of the book reflected in her eyes. She flipped to the next blank page, picked up her brush, wet it with fresh black ink, and brushed out her Chinese name, *Wu Chu Hua*.

She placed the brush down as she started to see the white light emanate from the Portal Book, and closed her eyes with a smile.

FOUR

The warm light cocooned Clara, who felt as if she'd been sailing smoothly through a bright expanse when she landed with a slight jolt.

"Clara!" she heard as she opened her eyes to see the Portal Book before her. She spun around to see Yuka smiling and walking briskly toward her. She was wearing a light-colored blouse tucked into a navy skirt, white socks that came up almost to her knees, along with her Azen shoes.

"Yuka!" said Clara gleefully as she embraced her.

As they parted, Yuka looked at Clara's tight activewear jacket.

"I love your jacket, it's so modern!" said Yuka.

"Thanks! I figured if I was going to practice my Kung Fu, I should have the right clothes," replied Clara.

"Welcome back, Empress Warrior Wu," said the Guardian Panda.

Clara's eyes lit up as she spun around with her mouth agape. She ran towards her Guardian Panda and buried herself into his thick white-and-black fur. He let out a low chuckle as he embraced her with his large paws.

"It's so good to see you, Guardian Panda!" said Clara as she pulled back. She then craned her neck, saw the other guardians, and greeted each one with a slight bow.

A panda attendant approached with a pair of shoes nestled on a soft red pillow.

"Shoes, Empress Warrior Wu," said the Guardian Panda.

"*Dò-jeh,*" said Clara excitedly as she put on the shoes.

"Hey!" said Daniel.

Clara and Yuka turned around to see Daniel smiling and waving at them. Before he walked over, he quickly greeted his Guardian Buffalo and bowed to each of the other guardians. He wore a grey long-sleeve athletic shirt and red shorts with double white stripes running down the sides. He was barefoot, and quickly put on his shoes offered by a buffalo attendant before jogging over to Clara and Yuka.

"Hi Daniel," said Yuka cheerily as Clara said, "Hey Scorch."

Daniel chuckled before he responded with, "Hey Quake."

"Looks like Sung is last again," said Yuka with a smirk. "I wonder what's he's doing?"

Clara and Daniel looked at each other and uttered, "StarCraft!" They both laughed as Yuka looked on silently.

"Empress warriors and emperor warrior," said the Guardian Panda as he stepped into the Portal Circle. "We'll continue to wait for Emperor Warrior Kim, in the meantime, feel free to talk amongst yourselves. While you wait, would you like anything to eat?"

"Oh, I'll just have some water," asked Clara.

"You wouldn't by any chance have *yaki onigiri*? It was almost dinner time and I'm a bit hungry," asked Yuka.

"Rice balls? I'm sure some can be brought out, Empress Warrior Satoh," said the Guardian Crane as she turned and gestured toward a crane attendant.

"*Domo arigato*," said Yuka with a slight bow.

"Emperor Warrior Nguyen, I believe we may have some fresh *gỏi cuốn* brought out for you as well," the Guardian Buffalo stated.

"Like spring rolls? That would be awesome!" said Daniel excitedly.

"And Empress Warrior Wu, I can have bamboo mushroom wontons in chili oil for you," said the Guardian Panda.

Clara's eyes lit up, "Okay. You talked me into it. *Dò-jeh!*"

"You're very welcome," said the Guardian Panda as he walked away along with the other guardians.

"Oh guys! I need to tell you about me and Clarissa!" exclaimed Clara.

"Did you kill her?" asked Daniel jokingly.

"No. I did not kill her," said Clara with a laugh.

Clara recapped her fight with Clarissa, but she was more excited to share how her parents defended her in front of the principal.

"And get this, my father said to me, 'I mean who do you think you are? Some kind of empress warrior?' I think my heart stopped," Clara said with a laugh along with Yuka and Daniel.

"Wow, your parents are pretty bad!" said Daniel.

"That's not very nice," said Yuka disapprovingly.

"What isn't very nice?" said Daniel with a puzzled look.

"To call her parents bad," said Yuka.

Daniel laughed, "Yuka, it doesn't mean they're bad literally. Like they are so bad, that they are actually good."

"I still don't think it's very nice," said Yuka as she crossed her arms.

"You're so cute sometimes, Yuka!" said Clara.

"I don't mean to be," said Yuka sheepishly.

"Oh! The food is here!" as Daniel spied the attendants coming toward the Portal Circle with trays.

They casually sat down in the Portal Circle with the lacquered trays set atop bamboo stands. They tore into the delicious foods and shared their food with each other.

"These dumplings are amazing!" said Clara. "They're almost as good as my mom's!"

"I hung out with my cousins last week and they are so impressed at how much better my Vietnamese is," said Daniel. "That really made me feel good."

"I'm so proud of you, Daniel," said Yuka reassuringly. "You should always take pride in your heritage. It's who you are. It's who we are."

"And the food is awesome!" said Daniel with a semi-mouthful of food.

"Ewww Daniel," exclaimed Clara. "Don't talk with your mouth full."

Daniel's expression turned to chuckled embarrassment as he closed his mouth and bowed for forgiveness.

"I've been manifesting a lot," said Yuka. "And I discovered new Qi elemental powers. Want to see?"

Clara's eyes lit up and said, "Sure."

Yuka smiled. "Okay, let's see if this is going to work as it'll be my first time invoking it."

Yuka looked around her and her fellow warriors. She invoked the Japanese word for *dome*, "*dōmu*," as she unfurled the bluish characters with a clenched fist, which she sent aloft. Everyone felt a gust of air expanding outward from her hand. In an instant, the ambient noise seemed muffled, but nothing else changed.

"What did you do?" asked Daniel as he looked around.

"Can you send up a small fire burst into the air?" asked Yuka. "A really small one."

Daniel invoked a small fire burst and sent it straight up. But it soon hit something invisible and splattered into streams that radiated outward and downward before extinguishing themselves.

"A dome!" said Yuka gently clapping. "I'm so glad it worked!"

"That's so cool!" said Clara. "So we're inside a dome of air?"

"Yep!" said Yuka gleefully. "I figured if we are surrounded by enemy creatures, I could cover us in a dome of air or drop a dome on top of our enemies. I was so frustrated how the *nues* were able to get around my air walls the last time."

Daniel shot up another fire burst as streams of fire gently flowed down along the dome's inner surface. Judging from where the split streams of fire ended on the ground, they were in a dome of air that was about ten feet in diameter and eight feet high. He looked at Yuka and asked teasingly, "So how do we get out of it?"

Yuka smiled, invoked the Qi element for evacuate, and the air dome collapsed.

"That is pretty cool," said Daniel. "How did you unlock more Qi elements?"

"I started to think of what else I could turn air into, besides a wall," said Yuka. "So I just tried to manifest different Japanese shapes, and *dōmu* manifested!

"I need to try that!" said Clara.

"I'll need to really work on my Vietnamese, then!" said Daniel excitedly.

"Empress warriors and emperor warrior," said the Guardian Tiger who strode up to them. "It looks like Emperor Warrior Kim will be a late arrival. I'll wait for him as you three are brought back to your respective kingdoms. Please take your weapons from your attendants."

"Thank you, Guardian Tiger," said Clara as Daniel and Yuka bowed slightly. They turned to receive their weapons from their respective attendants.

The three other guardians walked into the Portal Circle as several cranes and a pair of eagles descended from the sky to carry the guardians and the warriors back to their respective kingdoms.

"I'll see you guys tomorrow," said Clara as she walked toward the Guardian Panda. Upon reaching him, Clara looked at her crane as her beady eyes blinked at her.

"Welcome back, Empress Warrior Wu," said the crane.

"Shiori?" asked Clara with happiness.

"Yes," said Shiori. "Shall we fly?"

"You bet!" said Clara as she climbed aboard and harnessed herself in. They soon soared into the air with her Guardian Panda on the other crane.

"Empress Warrior Satoh," stated the Guardian Crane. Ready to fly back to Crane Castle?

"Ready," said Yuka as she climbed aboard her Guardian Crane. She gripped the harness and soon, flew off.

"Emperor Warrior Nguyen," said the Guardian Buffalo as Daniel looked in his direction. "Are we ready to fly back to the Palace of Divine Horns?"

Daniel looked to his side and gazed back at his Guardian Buffalo. He then asked, "Guardian Buffalo, would it be okay if I stopped by the Origins Pool first?"

The Guardian Buffalo's left eye widened a bit before it relaxed. "Certainly, we can do that for you, Emperor Warrior Nguyen. Would you like the eagle to take you there?"

"I can fly over there myself," said Daniel as he invoked a *thrust* Qi element. As he thrusted into the sky, he yelled down, "I'll be back soon."

"What is soon, Emperor Warrior…?" asked the Guardian Buffalo. But there was no response as Daniel flew out of earshot.

FIVE

The cool night air gently rushed against Clara's face as she watched the evening sky slowly dim and the sun set behind her. She looked up to see the stars and what she thought would be the third moon. Beautiful as it was, she shuddered a bit.

She felt Shiori starting to descend and saw Bamboo Tower in the distance. She smiled as she admired how the illumination jades bathed Bamboo City in a soft, green glow.

Shiori's wings fluttered to slow their speed as Clara looked over to the other crane. Her Guardian Panda was so cute, she thought, a joyful mound of white-and-black fur atop a majestic crane. He turned to her, blinked a few times, and gave a nod as she smiled back.

"Please hold onto your harness, Empress Warrior Wu," said Shiori. "We are now on final approach."

"Got it," said Clara as she regripped her harness and focused on the hangar opening. She saw a couple of pandas waving illumination jade batons to guide them in. Her eyes widened as her crane glided in with a loud swoosh, her mighty wings extended outward to slow her down before she settled onto her talons. Her wings folded neatly, and she lowered herself.

"*Domo Arigato!*" said Clara in her best Japanese for *thank you* as she carefully climbed down the beautiful feathers.

"*Dōitashimashite,*" said Shiori for *you're welcome* in Japanese as her beady eye blinked once at Clara.

Clara walked ahead of the crane to where the Guardian Panda was waiting for her. "You missed the flying, don't you?" he asked.

"I did," said Clara as she caught the Panderess and two of her attendants out of the corner of her eye. Clara turned to her, and the Guardian Panda took a step forward. They bowed courteously as the Panderess stopped a few feet away from them. She wore another beautiful red top with Chinese embroidery, along with a regal headdress made of bamboo. She also slightly bowed to Clara.

"Welcome back to Bamboo City, Empress Warrior Wu," said the Panderess as she smiled.

"Thank you," said Clara. "I wasn't expecting to see you in the hangar."

"I'm off to tend to a few duties," said the Panderess. "So, I just wanted to welcome you on your first day back before I missed the opportunity. Guardian Panda will see to your needs."

"*Xie Xie*," said Clara.

"Guardian Panda, I'll leave you to our Empress Warrior's needs for tonight. Have a good night," said the Panderess as she bowed slightly.

"Yes Panderess," said the Guardian Panda as he bowed along with Clara. "Have a good night."

The Panderess turned and walked gracefully away, followed by her two panda attendants.

Clara turned to the Guardian Panda and before she could say anything, her stomach emitted a loud growl. Embarrassed, Clara quickly covered her stomach and grinned sheepishly.

The Guardian Panda's eyes lit up as he grinned.

"Empress Warrior Wu," he said. "Usually, I would bring you up back up to your room here at Bamboo Tower, summon food for you, and let you retire for the night. But tonight, I was wondering if you'd like to have dinner with me and my family?"

Clara's eyes lit up in wonderment as she asked ebulliently, "You have a family?"

The Guardian Panda chuckled. "Yes, I have a wife and two young cubs."

"Oh cool! I would love to meet them!" said Clara ecstatically.

The Guardian Panda smiled and started walking toward the lift with Clara by his side. "Wonderful. I'll take you to your room and allow you to get changed."

"Sounds good," said Clara as she carefully stepped into the bamboo lift with the Guardian Panda.

The bamboo lift whisked upward and in no time, the Guardian Panda and Clara stepped off it. She was greeted by a couple of bowing panda attendants to whom she bowed in return.

"Empress Warrior Wu will be dining with me tonight," said the Guardian Panda. "Please help her select some appropriate evening clothing as I wait for her."

"Oh! I can find your home by myself," said Clara as she turned toward him.

The Guardian Panda's eyes lit up slightly before he replied, "Are you certain?"

"Yes," said Clara politely. "First number is the ring, second number is the bamboo stalk, and the last number is the floor."

"Your memory is impressive, Empress Warrior Wu," he said with amusement. "Certainly then. After you have changed, find my home at six, eight, ten. Do you have that?"

"Six, eight, ten…" said Clara. "Yes, I got that."

"Very well then," said the Guardian Panda. "If you get lost, just return here and any of the Bamboo Tower attendants can help you. I'll see you shortly."

"Okay!" said Clara as she watched the Guardian Panda turn and walk down the hallway out of sight.

"Empress Warrior Wu," said one of the panda attendants as Clara turned toward her. "We have laid out on your bed a couple of options for what you may wear tonight. Please let us know if you need anything more. We'll be right outside."

"*Dò-jeh!*" said Clara for *thank you* in Cantonese as she slightly bowed to both panda attendants.

Clara entered her room and smiled. The bamboo shutters were open, letting in cool, crisp air and she could see the darkening sky beyond The Ring as stars peeped through. She skipped toward her bed and saw a pant and a skirt outfit. She walked over to the wall and placed the Bow of Destiny upon the elegant rack with the quiver underneath it. Her eyes then went to the end table, and she knelt in front of it.

Her eyes fell onto the single bamboo stalk in a pebble-filled glass vase that the child panda, Ping Ping, had given to her during her last visit. She poured out a small amount of water from the bamboo water flask into the vase and looked at it fondly. It had grown since her last visit.

"I wonder if you'll grow to be just as amazing as the bamboo here in Bamboo City," said Clara under her breath. She smiled before she got up and began to change.

* * *

The bamboo lift came to a rest at the bottom of Bamboo Tower. Clara stepped out into the warm evening, wearing a new set of shoes, a bamboo-colored skirt and a short-sleeve pullover shirt with a V-neckline that was cinched in at the waist. The front edges of the V neckline had pretty, green edging with Chinese embroidery. She placed her hand on the Bow of Destiny's grip and looked down at the dim glowing Bamboo Jade and smiled. *It was still working,* she thought.

She looked outward and recited the Guardian Panda's address in her mind: "6 – 8 – 10." She walked down The Meridian and counted out the number of rings. She didn't expect the number of pandas she would encounter that night. As she walked up The Meridian, several pandas looked her way and bowed respectfully toward her, and she bowed in return. She would have entirely lost count had she not spotted the cute bamboo signs alit by illumination jades. She looked up and saw the sign in Chinese, "Ring 6. 1 – 50." She looked down when another male panda bowed to her as she bowed back.

She turned onto the sixth ring and strolled down the slightly curved path. Her eyes wandered upward as she took in the tall, green, jade-illuminated bamboo homes. Through the windows, she could see pandas going about their daily lives.

After counting out the bamboo homes, she believed she found the one that the Guardian Panda was living in. She looked at it and thought how funny it was that pandas lived in such large bamboo stalks. She smiled as she walked through the entrance and realized that she was stepping into a teahouse of some sort.

A pudgy panda strolling by stopped and glanced toward Clara with surprise before fully turning to her. Her paws went up to her face as she bowed graciously.

"Empress Warrior Wu!" she said. "I'm Mei Fan. May I help you with something?"

Clara bowed as she asked, "I'm here to see the Guardian Panda."

"Of course you are, he and his wonderful family live on the tenth floor of this bamboo," said Mei Fan with a big grin before her eyes, nestled in the black fur, flew open. "Oh, please wait here for one moment."

"Sure," said Clara curiously. She watched as Mei Fan waddled back behind her counter. She snatched up a pair of bamboo tongs and grabbed a paper bag in the other hand. She quickly tossed in several items with speedy panache. She sauntered her way back to Clara and handed her the bag with both of her paws.

Clara smiled, reached out for the bag, and asked, "Thank you. What are they?"

"My famous bamboo rice cake treats. They are crunchy and sweet. For you to bring as a gift to the Guardian Panda and his family. His cubs really enjoy them, and I hope you will too!"

"Thank you so much!" said Clara as she grinned graciously. "Could you tell me how I can get to the tenth floor?"

"Of course, Empress Warrior Wu," said Mei Fan. "Right where you came in, you'll find the entrance to the stairwell. It spirals through the entire outer bamboo wall."

"*Dò-jeh*," said Clara, for *thank you* in Cantonese, as she bowed and turned away from Mei Fan.

"Be sure to tell the Guardian Panda where you got the rice cakes from!" Mei Fan said as Clara left.

Clara found the stairwell entrance and her eyes brightened when she realized that the stairwell was carved into the thick outer wall of the bamboo itself. It was gently lit with illumination jades. She walked up the stairs, where all ambient sound from the outside was blocked until she came to each floor. Each floor had a bamboo door with a bamboo latch and above it was its numbered address in Chinese characters. The first one read, "6 – 8 – 2."

"Only eight more go," she mumbled to herself as she looked out of the window across from the door. She continued to climb the steps of the spiral bamboo staircase. By the time she reached the tenth floor, Clara had to rest against the bamboo wall and take a few breaths.

"Wow, that was some exercise," said Clara under her breath.

Clara straightened herself up and gently knocked on the door. She heard some shuffling from behind the door, and it opened. The Guardian Panda looked down at her with a smile and took a step back.

"Empress Warrior Wu," he said warmly. "Please come in, and welcome to my home."

Clara stepped through the door and entered a small area that was shielded by a curved bamboo wall.

"You may leave the Bow of Destiny and its quiver here," said the Guardian Panda. "It'll be safe."

"Oh, Guardian Panda," said Clara as she extended her hand with the fresh rice cakes. "Mei Fan from downstairs wanted me to give these to you."

The Guardian Panda's eyes lit up as he took the bag and opened it to reveal the rice cakes. The Guardian Panda gave Clara a sly look and said, "Best rice cakes in all of Bamboo City."

Clara slipped off her shoes and stepped onto a rough mat. She looked up at the Guardian Panda, who said, "That's to wipe our feet before we enter our homes. All panda homes have one."

Clara nodded as she followed him in. Her eyes panned the large circular room, befitting for a bamboo home. A slimmer panda looked up from what appeared to be a kitchen area. His wife, she surmised, as the second panda smiled and took off her apron.

"Clara, this is my wife, Bao Bao," said the Guardian Panda.

The Guardian Panda's wife came over and bowed to Clara.

"Empress Warrior Wu," she said in the warmest tone. "It is so warming to have you over for dinner. My husband has told me so much about you!"

"Thank you for having me!" said Clara excitedly. "Something smells delicious!"

"Yes!" said the Guardian Panda's wife. "Dinner is almost ready. Why don't you show her around?"

Just then, Clara's eyes shifted to the far end of the room, where plump balls of white-and-black fur were sliding down a pole from a hole in the ceiling. Clara gasped at the two adorable panda cubs, one larger than the other, scrambling toward her. But before they could barrel into her, the Guardian Panda stretched his arm toward them, and they froze as their eyes locked onto his glare.

"Cubblings, be respectful," said the Guardian Panda firmly. "Now I want you to say 'hello' respectfully."

The two adorable cubs got up on their feet, stood tall and in unison uttered, "Hello Empress Warrior Wu."

Clara bent down a bit and responded, "It's so nice to meet you! What are your names?"

The taller cub uttered, "I'm Mei Lun and this is…"

"I'm Mei Sheng," he said boldly as he looked up at his father. "Can I play with Empress Warrior Wu?"

Clara looked up at the Guardian Panda as her heart melted at how adorable the cubs were.

The Guardian Panda gave his two cubs a firm look and then relaxed, "Yes, you may, if it's okay with Empress Warrior Wu."

Clara smiled as the two panda cubs took each of her hands and led her away to their play area.

"Be careful with her," admonished the Guardian Panda as he chuckled.

The two panda cubs let go of Clara's hands and motioned for her to sit around a partially constructed structure made up of what appeared to be bamboo blocks.

The two cubs started to pick up pieces of bamboo and said, "Can you help us build Bamboo City?"

Clara looked down curiously and realized that the pieces were like a bamboo Lego set. She saw in front of her a scaled-down version of Bamboo City.

"Of course I will," said Clara happily as the panda cubs smiled back at her.

In the center of the collection of blocks, she saw Bamboo Tower measuring some six inches across and rising some three feet. Around it were several bamboo stalks in different states of completion. The completed bamboo stalks were about one inch in diameter and rose about two feet high.

Clara sat down and picked up two pieces to begin the puzzling task of assembling the bamboo sections. She saw that each section had a carved knob at the top and a hole at the bottom. Her hands came together to try to join the two pieces, but they did not fit together, even when she twisted them.

Mei Sheng caught Clara's attention, and she looked down at him with a smile.

"Not like that," said Mei Sheng as he reached out for the two pieces in Clara's hands.

Clara happily handed them over to Mei Sheng, who looked at each piece. He looked down at the floor and scanned the pieces before him, then suddenly lit up. He placed one piece down and picked up another, looking at the shape of the hole and of the knob of the other segment. He smiled as he successfully joined the two pieces. He extended them toward Clara, who took them with a smile.

"Like that," said Mei Sheng. "You need to find the knob that has the same shape as the hole."

"You are so smart," said Clara cheerfully.

Mei Sheng turned to his sister and whispered, "Empress Warrior Wu said I'm smart!" to which he giggled.

Clara smiled and looked down at all the jumbled pieces. She felt her heart melt as she watched how focused the panda cubs were trying to join the pieces together. Her hands gently rummaged through the pieces when it dawned on her that the correct pieces of a bamboo stalk had the same outer shape. She quickly placed the pieces in front of her with the knobs face up. Her actions did not go unnoticed as the panda cubs blinked curiously at what Clara was doing.

Clara focused on the pieces, and after finding about five more pieces for her already coupled bamboo sections, she was able to quickly add them onto her bamboo stalk. She was three sections short, and she broke off two sections and gave one to each cub. "Can you find me the remaining sections that are shaped like these?" asked Clara as she glided her finger over the shape of the bamboo cross section.

The cubs' eyes lit up with excitement as they started to paw through the pieces by placing everything face up and comparing them to the shape of the sections they already had. Mei Lun eagerly found two pieces, and Mei Sheng found the remaining piece. Clara's hands took them and soon snapped the pieces together to form a complete bamboo stalk.

"She's so fast!" exclaimed Mei Lun. "She is the Panda Warrior!"

Mei Sheng squealed in delight and Clara smiled with them.

"Can you find where my bamboo stalk goes?" asked Clara as she handed the bamboo stalk to Mei Sheng.

Mei Sheng took it, glanced at the bottom section, and read off the numbers ten and sixteen in Mandarin, "*shí, shí-liù.*" Mei Sheng quickly counted off ten rings from Bamboo Tower as Mei Lun counted the slots.

"Found it!" exclaimed Mei Lun with glee as her brother pressed it into place. When it snapped in, the cubs clapped their paws together.

"Why is the top section open?" asked Clara.

"Oh, that is to catch rainwater," said Mei Lun. "The section below is filled with stone to clean the rainwater. And the third section stores the clean water for our use."

Clara's eyes lit up at the elegant eco-friendly use of the bamboo home. "That's so resourceful!" said Clara.

"Dinner is ready, everyone," called the Guardian Panda's wife.

The cubs got up and taking Clara's hands, led her toward the round bamboo dinner table, which held numerous hot dishes that smelled familiar. The cubs pointed to her chair as the Guardian Panda watched slyly. Clara looked down at her seat and saw that it had a booster on it. She smirked at the Guardian Panda, who smiled back playfully. Clara took her seat as the cubs climbed onto their own boosted seats. The Guardian Panda and his wife soon sat down.

"I hope you'll enjoy the meal that I prepared, Empress Warrior Wu," said the Guardian Panda's wife. "My husband told me how much you enjoyed wontons in spicy chili oil, so I made my own today. Please try."

"They look delicious!" said Clara as she picked up a wonton with her chopsticks, blew on it, and plopped it into her mouth. Clara's eyes lit up in delight as she smiled and nodded in approval.

"Oh, I'm so glad you enjoy it," said the Guardian Panda's wife gleefully.

"Well then, let's eat," said the Guardian Panda as he picked up his chopsticks. His cubs did the same and expertly picked up their choice of food with their chopsticks.

Clara couldn't have envisioned a more unique experience: having dinner with a panda family.

SIX

Yuka let out a sigh as she marveled at the night sky passing by her as she nestled up against the warm feathers of her Guardian Crane.

"Are you tired, Empress Warrior Satoh?" asked her Guardian Crane.

"No," said Yuka. "It's just nice to be back."

"I see. We should be at Crane Castle soon."

"Can we fly a bit more?"

The Guardian Crane's beady eye rolled backward and then faced forward. "As you wish, Empress Warrior Satoh."

The Guardian Crane flapped her wings and steered right as the dark subtle waves below reflected the moons in the night sky.

"I manifested a lot of Qi elements when I was back home," said Yuka.

"It is good to be prepared," remarked the Guardian Crane.

"What kind of creatures will we be fighting this time?"

"I can't be certain, Empress Warrior Satoh," said the Guardian Crane. "The Warlock can summon up a variety of creatures, each with different abilities."

"Do we know where we will be fighting this time?"

As the Guardian Crane gazed forward, she responded, "It will be either north or south. Our aerial scouts will know once the third lunar eclipse has occurred."

Yuka spotted the third moon and wondered how something so beautiful could bring about so much destruction. She sighed.

"Guardian Crane?" Yuka asked.

"Yes?"

"How fast can you go?"

The Guardian Crane's beady eyes glanced backward before rolling forward and with a smile, quipped, "Very fast."

"Can I go as fast?" asked Yuka?

There was a pause as the Guardian Crane wondered for a moment before she answered, "I don't know, Empress Warrior Satoh. I've never raced a Crane Warrior before."

Yuka rose a bit and with a smile asked, "Want to see if I can catch up?"

There was a pause before the Guardian Crane asked, "Are you sure?"

"I am," said Yuka, playfully confident.

"Very well then, make yourself airborne and let's race the wind," the Guardian Crane encouraged.

With a gleeful expression, Yuka regripped the harness, got up into a crouch as she rested her soles atop the back of the Guardian Crane. She exhaled as the wind fluttered through her clothing.

"Ready, Empress Warrior Satoh?" asked the Guardian Crane as she stretched out her wings to steady herself.

"Ready," said Yuka with anticipation.

"Then, Empress Warrior Satoh, *jōshō suru!*" said the Guardian Crane in Japanese for *ascend!*

With a grin, Yuka let go of the harness and pushed off with her feet as she arced elegantly backwards into the air. She felt no fear as she welcomed the air and the freedom it provided her. Her body completed a flip as she glided through the wind.

The Guardian Crane flew alongside her and smiled as Yuka enjoyed an experience she couldn't indulge in back on Earth.

"Ready to see if you can keep up?" asked the Guardian Crane.

Yuka nodded, looked forward with a smile and with her right hand, invoked a *fly* Qi element as she shouted, *"Tobu!"* The Guardian Crane smiled and suddenly propelled herself ahead of Yuka.

Yuka smiled and willed herself to catch up to her Guardian Crane. Surprisingly, she caught up and was soon alongside the Guardian Crane once more. But the Guardian Crane simply smiled and with a few strong flaps, was again ahead of Yuka.

Yuka smiled and felt the exhilaration of the chase. She followed on the tail of the Guardian Crane and noticed how she pulled her wings and talons close to her body, giving her an aerodynamic advantage.

Following her lead, Yuka pulled her arms closer, tucked in her chin and willed herself on to catch up. Suddenly, the Guardian Crane executed some beautiful aerial spirals. Yuka did the same and felt the wind spindle along her entire body. Before she could straighten out, the Guardian Crane shot upward, and Yuka followed. The Guardian Crane was indeed fast, but Yuka wasn't far behind. She didn't care if she was faster or not, she just wanted to fly with the majestic Guardian Crane.

Soon, the Guardian Crane slowed down and Yuka flew alongside her.

"That was wonderful!" said Yuka with a big grin on her face.

"Your flying skills are admirable, Empress Warrior Satoh," the Guardian Crane extolled.

"Not too bad for a Japanese American girl from Arizona," said Yuka.

"Yes… what is Arizona?"

Yuka giggled.

"Back to Crane Castle?" asked the Guardian Crane.

Yuka nodded as she invoked another fly Qi element. The Guardian Crane gracefully banked left and flew underneath Yuka. She followed the Guardian Crane toward Crane Castle.

SEVEN

Calm descended on the Azen night as the Guardian Buffalo trudged carefully along the path toward the Origins Pool. The tall bamboo lined the path as his eyes softly glowed red. At the end of the path, the Guardian Buffalo looked up and saw Daniel sitting against the low stone wall of the Origins Pond. Daniel had hinted he wanted to be left alone, and the Guardian Buffalo had agreed, but that was more than an hour ago.

Though the Guardian Buffalo did not want to intrude on his emperor warrior, it was getting late, and it was his duty to get Daniel back to the Palace of Divine Horns. He let out a soft grunt and walked toward Daniel as quietly as possible, but given his massive weight, anything under his hooves crackled. But Daniel did not seem to hear the rustling of crushed bamboo and leaves and was still staring into the calm waters of the Origins Pool.

As he neared, the Guardian Buffalo uttered gently, "Emperor Warrior Nguyen."

Daniel raised his gaze toward the Guardian Buffalo with teary eyes, which he wiped with his long sleeve. Upon seeing Daniel's sadness, the Guardian Buffalo briskly closed the remaining steps.

"Emperor Warrior Nguyen, what is the matter?" he asked.

Daniel collected himself, wiped his nose along his sleeve once more. He sniffled while shaking his head. "It's nothing, I'm fine," feigned Daniel in response.

"It can't be fine. Why are you sad?"

Daniel looked down and subtly nodded toward the water of the Origins Pool.

The Guardian Buffalo turned toward the calm water. His right ear fluttered as he looked at a bald man in a short-sleeved sports jersey, sporting sunglasses with uneven stubble across his face. He was sitting back in a lawn chair holding a beer, with a swimming pool reflected in his sunglasses.

"Who is this?" asked the Guardian Buffalo.

"That's my father," said Daniel with contempt. "That's the one that called me a *gook*."

The Guardian Buffalo turned back to Daniel and asked, "Why did he call you *country*?"

Puzzled, Daniel looked up and uttered, "Huh?

"*Gook*," said the Guardian Buffalo. "It sounds like country in Chinese or Korean."

Surprised, Daniel asked, "It does? Wait, you speak Chinese and Korean?"

The Guardian Buffalo stared at Daniel and said subtly, "I've been with my fellow guardians for some time now. I've picked up enough of their respective languages to understand them."

"Oh, that makes sense," said Daniel. "Well, where I'm from, it's a mean word said by a person of another race to an Asian person, to make them feel bad."

"What is race?"

"Oh, that's one group of people that look like each other versus another group of people who also look similar. Like I'm Asian and he's White."

The Guardian Buffalo looked back at the image of Daniel's father and looked back at Daniel. "I believe you are mistaken, he's not white."

"Um, yes he is," said Daniel.

The Guardian Buffalo turned back to Daniel. "He looks more pink to me."

Daniel looked back at his father and noticed his slight sunburn and let out a laugh. "Pink! Maybe you are right, he does look kind of pink."

The Guardian Buffalo stared at Daniel and didn't know why Daniel laughed. As Daniel chuckled, he stepped closer to the edge of the Origins Pool and stared at Daniel's father for a few seconds before turning back. "There are some parts of him that I see in you."

"Don't say that, Guardian Buffalo!" said Daniel agitatedly. "This is the same man that left my *mẹ* and me because he hated the Vietnamese in me. Like what did he think he was going to get when he married my mother? A dark-haired White boy?"

"No," said the Guardian Buffalo flatly. "He got the Emperor Warrior of the Buffalo Kingdom."

Daniel smiled and looked up at the Guardian Buffalo, "You always know what to say."

"You're welcome, Emperor Warrior Nguyen," said the Guardian Buffalo.

"Is this the first time you've seen a White... I mean a pink man?"

"Yes, I believe so," said the Guardian Buffalo. "You are the first halfling we've ever had in Azen."

Daniel nodded and turned up toward the Guardian Buffalo. "I see. I promise to work twice as hard because I'm only half."

The Guardian Buffalo looked down on Daniel and asked, "What do you mean by that?"

"Well since I'm only half Vietnamese, I know I have to work twice as hard as the others. It's what you've always been telling me, to work twice as hard."

"Young Emperor Warrior Nguyen," said the Guardian Buffalo as he shifted his massive body toward Daniel. "I think you misunderstood me."

Daniel turned toward the Guardian Buffalo with a puzzled expression and asked. "What do you mean?"

The Guardian Buffalo gazed into Daniel's moonlit eyes. "When I said you have to work twice as hard, I meant it to mean that you have to work twice as hard to overcome the belief that you are not Vietnamese. Your Vietnamese spirit courses through your blood, but you yourself did not fully embrace it until you arrived here on Azen. The Portal Book chose you because you are Vietnamese of heart, even if you don't know it yet."

Daniel's glassy eyes looked confused as he looked about him before he looked back at the Guardian Buffalo and asked, "But what makes my Vietnamese spirit so strong?"

The Guardian Buffalo's brown-reddish eyes blinked and looked deeply at Daniel as he asked, "Do you not know?"

With a blank look yearning for the answer, Daniel shook his head.

"Your mother, Emperor Warrior Nguyen," said the Guardian Buffalo. "Your mother's Vietnamese love for you is strong."

Daniel's lips trembled as he brought his hand to his heart and looked up and uttered, "My *mẹ*?"

The Guardian Buffalo nodded his head.

Daniel's eyes filled up with tears as he stared at the Guardian Buffalo before his head dipped as he sobbed copiously. The Guardian Buffalo stepped forward, gently placed his forehead on Daniel's head and held it there as Daniel sobbed.

EIGHT

"And his two cubs were so adorable!" said Clara excitedly to Yuka.

"You got to play with them?" said Yuka. "Did they crawl all over you like how baby pandas would?"

"No," said Clara. "They were well behaved. I think it's because they are toddlers."

"*Buổi sáng tốt lành!*" said Daniel in Vietnamese for *good morning* as he walked into the Portal Circle.

Yuka's eyes lit up as she exclaimed, "Daniel, why are your eyes all puffy?"

Daniel stopped in his tracks and noticed that Clara gasped as she started at him. He quickly wiped his sleeve across his eyes and put on a broad smile. "Oh! I mistakenly ate a really hot pepper last night with my dinner," he said.

"That must have been a really hot pepper," said Clara who let out a sigh of relief. "You must be really careful, some of the Asian peppers are really hot."

Relieved that Clara and Yuka believed him, Daniel feigned acknowledgement and said, "Yes, you are so right. I need to ask about the peppers before I eat them next time."

"You're lucky you're half Vietnamese," said Yuka smartly. "It's probably what saved you from that pepper."

"Yah! You're probably right," said Daniel with a chuckle as he started to get hot under his collar. That's when he saw a glowing light from the corner of his eye.

The bright light enveloped everything around the water Wu Portal Book. As Sung appeared in the Portal Circle, he was forced to squint until the brightness subsided. He felt a slight jolt and exhaled as he opened his eyes. He saw the steely blue eyes of the Guardian Tiger staring back at him.

"Welcome back, Emperor Warrior Kim," the Guardian Tiger greeted him.

"Guardian Tiger! *Annyeonghaseyo!*" said Sung with excitement.

"Finally!" exclaimed Clara with a hint of annoyance as Sung turned toward his friends. He was about to saunter off when the Guardian Tiger grunted.

Sung quickly turned around to see the Guardian Tiger motion toward a tiger attendant, who had a pair of shoes for him. Sung looked down at his bare feet and grinned sheepishly as he ran back toward the tiger attendant. Sung bowed as he snatched the shoes from the tiger attendant and uttered, "*gam-sa-ham-ni-da.*"

After placing on his shoes, Sung sauntered over to his friends, who looked exasperated. "Oh man! Am I the last one again?"

Clara replied with displeasure, "Yes."

"StarCraft?" asked Daniel.

Sung turned to Daniel with annoyance, "Not this time. I was, well, helping my father prep for his Tae Kwan Do class."

"That's great!" said Yuka supportively.

"Yah," said Sung as he swayed his head a bit. "It's the first time I spent a whole day with my *appa,* and he seemed so happy that I was helping him."

"You don't think he knows you're like a Tae Kwan Do master by now?" asked Clara.

"Oh no," said Sung as his eyes smiled. "He knows I'm much better than before, but I'm holding back. He doesn't say it, but I think he's proud of me."

"I'm sure he is," said Clara.

"I hope so," said Sung with a nod.

The Guardian Tiger had silently walked up to them and caught their attention with a soft growl. "Emperor Warrior Kim, would you like some food or something to drink?"

"I'm good, Guardian Tiger," said Sung as he bowed his head slightly. "I just came back from the *dojang,* and when I went back to my room, I saw the Portal Book glowing."

"*Dojang?*" asked Daniel.

"That is Korean for *training hall*," said the Guardian Tiger. "Very well then, I see that the other guardians are returning. Please stand by your Portal Books."

Sung nodded as he and the others walked back to their Portal Books just as the other guardians met their emperor or empress warriors. The emperor and empress warriors faced inward, with Sung looking out of place in his clothes from home and everyone else in their training attire. The Guardian Tiger circled about the center before rising onto his hind legs. With the blue jade about his neck aglow, he summoned from Sung's Portal book streams of fire that wove themselves into an image of the Azen terrain.

The streams of flames reflected in the eyes of the warriors as the Guardian Tiger spoke. "We have conquered two of the Warlock's armies, the *Huo Dou* demon dogs and the *nues*, in the east and the west. That means the next battle will be either to the north or the south. Both are treacherous, as the north is a sea battle, and the south is a rocky canyon battle."

"Yes?" asked the Guardian Tiger when he saw Sung raise his hand.

"How soon until the next battle?" he asked.

The Guardian Tiger looked up into the morning sky and barely made out the third moon. He lowered his hand and in low tone said, "It may be in three or five days."

"The next lunar eclipse will occur three days from now," said the Guardian Tiger. "If the Warlock's army spawns to the north, the battle will begin later that day. But if they spawn to the south, it will be two days after the lunar eclipse." The Guardian Tiger exited the Portal Circle, allowing the Guardian Panda to enter.

The Guardian Panda waved the fiery streams away and summoned from Clara's Portal Book new fiery streams that wove into a large jade that represented the Bamboo Jade in Clara's bow.

"Emperor and empress warriors," started the Guardian Panda. "My fellow guardians, the leaders of our kingdoms and experts had long discussions while you were away. We have noticed that your experiences here were a bit different than those of previous empress and emperor warriors. For example, in all our history, when the warriors' jades were employed, never has one shattered, rendering its power obsolete. This is what happened to Empress Warrior Wu's Bamboo Jade. So it is important that you do your best to protect your jades. I am sure that this bit of news has gotten back to the Warlock. Is that understood?"

As the Guardian Panda circled about making eye contact with Sung, Yuka, Daniel, and finally Clara, they all silently nodded in grave understanding.

"The other unexpected anomaly," continued the Guardian Panda, "was how Clara's earthen jade awakened and powered up the green jade attached to the pandas' battle armor at Jagged Pass."

Clara pursed her lip as she glided her right hand over the jade bracelet on her left wrist. She felt its coolness and glanced down as it glistened for a moment under the morning sun. She looked back up.

"Though we do not know how this occurred," said the Guardian Panda with a sobering tone. "We are thankful for whatever latent powers it had to help us in our time of need."

The Guardian Panda waved away the fiery streams that made up the Bamboo Jade and they reassembled into the beautiful Korean nine-tailed fox, the *gumiho* that had seduced Sung.

Daniel snickered at Sung and gestured upward at the representation of the *gumiho* as he mouthed to Sung, "She's hot."

Sung, visibly annoyed, gave Daniel an expression of irritation, shooing him away with a flick of his hand as he focused on the Guardian Panda.

"The nine-tailed fox, known as a *kitsune* in Japanese, *huli jing* in Chinese and of course…" the Guardian Panda paused as he turned to Sung. "*Gumiho* in Korean."

Sung looked down at his shoes and uttered, "Must you remind me, Guardian Panda?"

The Guardian Panda smirked and continued. "Over our history, shape shifters, such as the *gumiho*, have often wandered into the Azen realm, to either spy or sabotage our plans. We are more familiar with their ways and can spot them. But the power of the jade acts as a deterrent to their spells and manipulations. We do not know how they can come into our land, but as they are mystical creatures, they have powers that are beyond our understanding. So it is important that you always carry your jade with you. Is that clear?"

Clara, Daniel, and Yuka nodded as the Guardian Panda made eye contact with them. He then settled his gaze on Sung, who nodded as well before the Guardian Panda waved off the fiery streams representing the cunning and seductive *gumiho*.

The Guardian Buffalo entered the Portal Circle as the Guardian Panda stepped out.

The massive body of the Guardian Buffalo made a light thud with each of his steps, and he circled about before settling his gaze on Daniel.

"Emperor and empress warriors," said the Guardian Buffalo. "As you have now been victorious in two battles, it is important that you continue to manifest your Qi elements. Also, continue to try to unlock Qi elements by trying new words. By having an arsenal of Qi elements, it will better arm you for the battles ahead."

Everyone nodded.

"Very well. Why don't you begin manifesting and hopefully you can discover new Qi elements."

Everyone nodded as Clara, Sung, Yuka, and Daniel turned toward their Portal Books. They picked up their brushes and started to manifest away.

NINE

"Wow! I so missed Azen food!" exclaimed Sung, rubbing his belly as he walked toward the Portal Circle with Daniel at his right.

Daniel nodded as his stomach strained to digest all the food he had just devoured. Both his and Sung's appetites were befitting of two growing teenage boys.

Clara and Yuka walked arm in arm trailing them by about ten feet away.

"Do you think I can see the panda cubs too?" asked Yuka.

"I'm sure Guardian Panda won't mind," said Clara warmly. "Maybe between now and the eclipse?"

"Mmmm," said Yuka in agreement. "Pandas are so cute! I wonder if the cranes have baby chicks?"

Both Clara and Yuka giggled at the thought as they reached the Portal Circle. They separated and went to their respective Portal Books with their guardians already standing by them.

The Guardian Crane entered the Portal Circle, and her beady eyes blinked a few times.

"Empress and emperor warriors," the Guardian Crane stated. "I hope you enjoyed lunch. I know the emperor warriors did, as I haven't seen two boys eat so much food at one sitting."

Both Sung and Daniel smiled and bashfully looked away.

"Very well, then," continued the Guardian Crane. "As we just finished a large meal, let's begin our training with something light. Let's see what new Qi elements you have discovered. As this will be the first time you are invoking them, please use them lightly. Who would like to go first?

"I'll go!" volunteered Sung with his hand raised up energetically.

"Very well, then. You may proceed, Emperor Warrior Kim," said the Guardian Crane.

Sung looked at everyone and brushed into the air as he whispered in Korean, "*nun.*"

Clara suddenly looked up in awe as soft snow started to fall from the sky. They floated down gently and Clara, along with everyone, reached up for the snowflakes.

"Beautiful!" exclaimed Yuka as she tilted her head backwards to try to catch a snowflake on her tongue.

That's when Sung invoked another Qi element and suddenly, the snow turned to a light rain, startling everyone as the cool rain fell upon them.

"Sung!" hollered Clara as she wrapped her arms about her shoulders. But the rain subsided and Clara looked over at Yuka, who had just invoked a dome of air over the entire Portal Circle.

Everyone looked up as the rain drops hit the dome and gently slid down its sides. The raindrops turned into a light snow that fell onto the dome. Clara looked up, mesmerized by the white flakes falling silently onto the dome of air. But that silence was quickly replaced by quick pops, which echoed unrelentingly as hail pelted the dome. The quick transition startled Clara, but soon she found the sight and sound of the hail hitting and bouncing off the dome oddly satisfying. She looked at Yuka, who was smiling up at the airy display. Then it all stopped as Sung invoked a Qi element to evaporate the hail.

"That's dope!" exclaimed Daniel. "My turn."

Daniel invoked a small orb of fire that floated in front of him. He smiled at its size and its proximity to him. He was warmed by the heat as it helped to dry off his training attire. He invoked similar orbs of fire that floated in front of his fellow warriors and guardians.

Clara reached out for the floating orb of fire, just barely grazing it with her fingertips. She was mesmerized by it. The heat that it gave off was warm and inviting. But suddenly, the gentle heat started to flow toward her and felt even warmer. Clara looked at Yuka, who had just invoked a Qi element herself. "*Toppū!* Gust! I created a small gust of wind in front of each fire that Daniel created," Yuka exclaimed joyfully.

"Excellent!" extolled the Guardian Crane. "You three have not only discovered new Qi elements, but also mastered your control of them. Excellent. Now that we are sufficiently warmed up, Empress Warrior Satoh, please stop the gust of wind. Emperor Warrior Nguyen, please extinguish the small fires. And Empress Warrior Satoh, please release the dome. In that order, please."

Yuka and Daniel neutralized their Qi elements before returning to attention. The Guardian Crane turned to Clara and asked, "And what of you, Empress Warrior Wu?"

Clara let out a sigh and said, "It's not as cute as the other three, but I can do this."

Clara looked to her right, beyond Daniel and brushed through the air as she said, *"jum doong,"* Cantonese for *tremor.* The bluish Chinese character emerged at her fingertips, and she cast it out gently as it sank into the ground. Immediately, the ground behind Daniel shook for a few seconds.

"Whoa!" exclaimed Daniel. "Good job, Quake."

"I think that was on low," said Clara smugly. "Now watch this."

Clara invoked the Chinese character for tremor once more and cast it into the ground behind Daniel. The dirt behind Daniel rippled in small waves that spread about a hundred feet.

Daniel returned his gaze to Clara along with everyone else, and they nodded their heads in approval. "Tremors like that can make it tough for the advancing enemy," Daniel said.

"Excellent work, empress and emperor warriors," said the Guardian Crane approvingly. "For the remainder of the day, we will work with you to explore other Qi elements and help you refine them. We will also help you understand, from our battle experience, when certain Qi elements will be more applicable. Please pair up with your guardians and let's get to work. Empress Warrior Satoh, please come with me."

As Yuka followed the Guardian Crane out of the Portal Circle, she looked up at her winged guardian.

"Guardian Crane?" Yuka began.

"Yes, Empress Warrior Satoh?" she replied.

"Do you have any chicks?"

The Guardian Crane stopped on her talons and looked down at Yuka bewildered. "How do you mean, Empress Warrior Satoh?"

Yuka looked up innocently, "You know, do you have any children?"

The Guardian Crane's beady eyes blinked and then closed as she let out some quick squawks. She looked down at Yuka and responded, "Why yes, Empress Warrior Satoh, I do. I have one young teen crane. He is quite the eager one."

Yuka smiled and asked, "Can I meet him?"

The Guardian Crane smiled and replied, "Why certainly, Empress Warrior Satoh. It would be my honor for you to meet him."

Yuka nodded her head happily and let out, "Great!"

TEN

The next day at lunch, Sung was plowing rice into his mouth from the metal rice bowl and snapping up the variety of Korean *ban chan* dishes set before him. Daniel was doing the same, trying to satisfy his voracious appetite. As Daniel gulped down a mouthful of rice, he eyed the last slice of *kimchi* pancake and went in to grab it with his chopsticks, only to be blocked by Sung's chopsticks. Daniel looked up at Sung, who looked back at him as a few pieces of rice were in between his lips.

Sung smiled, chuckled, and pulled away his chopsticks and motioned with his chopsticks toward Daniel. Daniel smiled back and pulled away his chopsticks, making the same motion to Sung. Sung refused, nodded and Daniel smiled, nodded. They stared at each other when they both moved in with their chopsticks that collided as they gave each other a surprised look.

"Share!" snapped Clara as she looked at them with playful annoyance. She waved off their chopsticks, reversed her chopsticks and cleanly split the last slice of *kimchi* pancake. Her eyes looked at the hungry teenaged boys as her eyes said, "go."

Both Sung and Daniel nodded at Clara, and they each took up the halved slice of *kimchi* pancake. As they brought it to their lips, a tiger attendant came in behind Clara and Yuka, removed the empty plate, and replaced it with a new warm plate of *kimchi* pancake. Both Sung and Daniel stared at the new plate when both Clara and Yuka snatched up a slice for themselves. Clara and Yuka grinned at each other.

Their morning was spent manifesting their newfound powers and testing out their expanding Qi elemental powers. Sung created a larger-than-expected blizzard that forced Yuka to create a large dome of air to shield them. Daniel created a larger-than-expected floating orb of fire that traveled outside of the Portal Circle, causing the Guardian Panda and Tiger to leap away. Clara's tremor rippled the earth and bounced the seemingly immovable Guardian Buffalo off his hooves, embarrassingly tipping him onto his side. They ended their afternoon just as dinner came around.

"Guardian Buffalo," asked Daniel as he finished up his last bite of a *kimchi* pancake.

"Yes, Emperor Warrior Nguyen?" asked the Guardian Buffalo as his large brown eyes peered down at Daniel.

"I was wondering, instead of waiting for the Warlock's armies to come to Azen, could we bring the fight to them?"

The Guardian Buffalo put down his bowl and chopsticks and said in steady voice, "No, it's not practical. As mentioned before, the land that separates Azen and Nadi, which we call The Shards, is a glassy terrain filled with deep fissures and crevasses. Only by air is it traversable. Besides, we could never leave our kingdoms defenseless."

"Have you ever tried to cross it?" asked Daniel as the other warriors listened attentively.

"Long ago, regiments of battle soldiers from our kingdoms tried. But it was futile, as the land was not merciful. The terrain itself is glasslike. Though the crystal-like terrain seemed solid, it is unforgivingly brittle. It was hard on the paws and hooves of those soldiers who fell to their deaths in the crevasses when the glass shattered. The strange thing about The Shards is that the glass seems to grow back. New crevasses would be filled again with the obsidian-like material the next day."

"Well, how about flying?" asked Daniel.

The Guardian Buffalo looked at the Guardian Crane, who turned to Daniel.

"Emperor Warrior Nguyen," said the Guardian Crane gravely. "We also have tried that. We have sent out many cranes for reconnaissance. Many of them did return, so we've mapped out much of the treacherous land between Azen and Nadi. Reaching the Warlock's fortress is even possible by flight within a few hours. But something inexplicable happened on one reconnaissance mission. Our reconnaissance squadron was able to locate the Warlock's fortress. With our eyes, we can see long distances. That same squadron, after a day's rest in Azen, flew again to attempt to reach the Warlock's fortress for a closer look. It never returned. A rescue squadron was sent in, but they too never returned. After the third rescue squadron did not return, it was forbidden by decree by the Azen Council to make further attempts to reach the Warlock's fortress."

"But it's different now," said Daniel. "We have Clara who can whip up a wall of dirt to cross the chasms…"

"Emperor Warrior Nguyen, that won't work, as there is no discernible earth across The Shards," the Guardian Buffalo interjected.

"Well, we've got Sung then, he can easily create ice bridges," offered Daniel.

"The ice bridges would melt over time, and their weight could fracture The Shards," said the Guardian Buffalo as his brown eyes furrowed.

"He can just recreate them on the way back," replied Daniel.

"Assuming nothing happens to him," said the Guardian Buffalo tersely.

"Nothing will happen to him, I have his back…" said Daniel confidently when he was taken aback by the Guardian Buffalo's hoof slamming atop the communal meal table; rattling every dish, plate, cup and chopstick.

Silence fell onto the table as the Guardian Buffalo glared at Daniel.

"Emperor Warrior Nguyen!" snapped the Guardian Buffalo as he beamed at Daniel, who shrunk back in his seat. "Enough! By decree, we are forbidden to travel to the land of Nadi. We will respect the will of the Azen Council. Do I make myself clear?"

Daniel looked petrified as he nodded. He had never seen the Guardian Buffalo mad at him.

"I'm sorry, Guardian Buffalo," Daniel beseeched. "I did not mean to anger you or disrespect you or the other guardians."

The Guardian Buffalo relaxed his snarled face and his hoof upon the table as he let out a snort. "Besides, there is one other important factor that would be a disadvantage. While across The Shards, the power of the jade seems to be neutralized."

"Oh," said Yuka as silence enshrouded the meal table.

"Emperor Warrior Nguyen," said the Guardian Buffalo softly. "I did not mean to be angry with you. For that I am sorry. I know you meant well, but just know, previous generations have already tried what you suggested. But what we do know is that we have won each battle with the Warlock's army on our own terrain. That is how it's always been and will be."

Daniel nodded and he saw his fellow warriors looking uncomfortable as they went back to slowly eating their food. Daniel looked down into the metal rice bowl and started to pick at the last bits of food while thoughts of the Warlock's fortress lingered.

ELEVEN

Clara gazed at her battle armor in her tent quarters as the evening set in. She admired the grayish chest plate with its contoured green jade dust inlay pattern, the shoulder plates, the interlocked waist armor, the thigh guards, the forearm gauntlets, and the boots. She couldn't wait to put it on once more.

She turned as she heard the flap to her tent open and saw Sung entering cautiously.

Clara suddenly perked up as she closed the wardrobe, brushed her hair aside and said, "Sung."

"Oh, hey, there you are," said Sung sheepishly as he straightened up and took a few steps toward Clara.

"What's up?"

"Not much," began Sung as he fidgeted slightly before he recomposed himself. "That was a scene earlier, right? With Daniel getting the Guardian Buffalo all mad."

"Yah," said Clara. "I've never seen the Guardian Buffalo that mad before. I hope I never get my Guardian Panda that mad."

"Or my Guardian Tiger," said Sung as he smirked before an awkward pause set in.

Clara looked up curiously at Sung and as she pursed her lips, she asked, "Did you come into my tent to ask me that?"

Sung grinned as he ran his fingers through his hair and then looked down at Clara. "Well no, I kinda came to get you because Daniel and Yuka was going to head to the Origins Pool and I wanted to see if you wanted to come too."

Clara feigned a cheery tone as she responded, "Sure, sounds like fun. Let me get my bow."

"Cool," said Sung as he watched Clara turn away from him and toward the bamboo stand. She picked up the quiver and slung it over her back as the jade-tipped arrows rattled slightly. Her hand grasped the bow, and she slung it across her chest. Lastly, she reached down for the illumination jade torch and spun around.

"Okay, let's go," Clara said warmly.

* * *

Clara walked along the path toward the Origins Pool, which was lined with the familiar bamboo stalks. Their footsteps were quiet except for the occasional crack of a fallen bamboo stalk being stepped on. They were nearing the end of the path when Clara looked up and saw Daniel and Yuka. She was sitting on the stone slab encircling the Origins Pool as Daniel sat close by on the ground with a jade torch between them.

Clara smiled as she moved out of the path, followed close behind by Sung.

"Hey guys," said Clara as she waved to them with the jade torch.

"Hey Clara," said Yuka as Daniel twisted and nodded at her. He seemed at ease after his beratement by the Guardian Buffalo.

Clara bounded up to Yuka and sat behind her as she twisted her jade torch shut.

Sung stepped up to them, sat on the stone slab, and exhaled. "What a nice night," he said as he gazed up into the night sky.

"It's always nice here," said Yuka.

"I wonder what other pools are out there and what cool properties they have?" said Sung just as Daniel glanced discreetly at Clara. "Have the guardians told you about any other pools?" asked Sung.

Clara cast a look at Daniel and shook her head slightly before she spoke up. "Not that I'm aware of."

Clara didn't feel good about telling a fib but felt that the experience with the truth pools within the Jade Labyrinth were personal. Daniel settled his gaze upon his friends as he gently slid the club horn away from him so that he could look down into the red jade.

"Hey, so I just wanted to say," Daniel started as he broke his gaze into the red jade and looked up at everyone. "I didn't mean to make you guys feel uncomfortable at lunch."

Sung looked at Yuka's and Clara's blank faces before looking back up at Daniel, "Don't worry about it, bro."

"I really do wonder what happened to the crane squadrons that went out and never came back," said Yuka. "It makes me sad to know that they never returned."

"It makes you curious, doesn't it?" asked Daniel.

"It happened so long ago," said Sung. "They did what they thought was right at the time. But now, the cranes prepare for each battle like the others, and as their warriors, we give them a huge advantage."

"I wish they didn't have to fight," said Yuka sorrowfully.

"I wonder if we could somehow learn more about the Warlock?" asked Daniel.

Everyone looked up before Clara asked, "What do you mean?"

Daniel gently nodded in the direction of the serene Origins Pool, causing everyone to look towards it. They turned back toward Daniel looking perplexed.

"But we can't summon the Warlock," said Clara.

"Not the Warlock," said Daniel as he gazed upon Sung. "Jisoo."

Sung's eyes widened. "Huh? What?"

"Hear me out," said Daniel. "These pools of water are amazing mystical things. I don't even think our guardians know exactly how they work."

"That's pretty arrogant of you to say," said Clara sternly. "All of a sudden, you know more than our guardians?"

"Yah, that's not nice," said Yuka.

Daniel shook his head. "That came out all wrong. What I'm saying is, the Origins Pool has mystical powers and maybe we need to test them in other ways. To see if they can do other things."

"So why did you look at me?" asked Sung.

"Well maybe you can summon her, and we can see where she is," said Daniel.

"Hold on," Clara interjected. "Our guardians told us that the Origins Pool can only show our parents. The *gumiho* is not Sung's parent."

"Totally not!" Sung injected vehemently.

"Yah but the *gumiho* sucked out his Qi, so she knows him pretty intimately," said Daniel.

"Bro! That just creeps me out!" said Sung with revulsion.

"Hey, I'm not saying it will work. But what if somehow you and her are connected now because of your Qi?" asked Daniel.

"I have to admit," said Clara slowly. "I'm kinda intrigued."

"Oh great," stammered Sung. "You want me to summon the *gumiho* too?"

"Come on, Sung," Daniel entreated. "If we could find something out that would help our guardians and the kingdoms, wouldn't that be worth it?"

Sung withdrew a bit as everyone's eyes fell on him. He looked out over the calm water and then back at Daniel.

"Fine, I'll try," said Sung reluctantly. "But just this once. I'm already creeped out by this."

"Cool!" exclaimed Daniel as he crouched down to Sung's left.

Everyone else got onto their knees and leaned over the stone slab with curiosity and trepidation. Daniel leaned the club horn up against the low stone wall as Sung placed the Claw Staff onto the stone slab.

"Okay, so what do I do?" asked Sung rhetorically.

"Just like how you brought up your parents but this time, think of Jisoo. Because she's hot," said Daniel teasingly.

Sung gave Daniel a stern side look as he raised the back of his hand towards Daniel's head, "I should smack you right about now!"

Daniel pulled back with a disarming smile, holding his hands up. Sung brought his hand back down as he shook his head. Clara and Yuka smirked.

Sung placed his thumb on the blue jade, leaned over and dipped his left hand into the cool water. He closed his eyes and thought of Jisoo with dread. He stayed that way for a few seconds, as a fleeting beautiful memory of her appeared in his mind before he withdrew his hand and opened his eyes.

Everyone looked at the still dark blue water.

"Nothing is happening," whispered Clara.

"Yah, I don't think anything is gonna happen," said Sung.

"Wait!" said Yuka, pointing at the pool with a jittery hand.

Everyone looked. A blurry image started to form in the dark water. Gentle waves appeared out of nowhere, moving toward them. A dark, ethereal image appeared in each ripple and started to form as the waves flattened out. The backside of a slim woman with nine fluffy fox-like tails started to crystalize. Her black hair was ravenous and flowing. Another figure appeared to her right, and two other figures to her left.

"That's the *gumiho*," whispered Clara as she pointed with her mouth slightly agape.

"Jisoo," said Sung as he looked at her, mesmerized by her, yet resentful of her.

"Yes, we know, your girlfriend. But that's the Ox Head Demon Lord from the first battle," whispered Daniel in awe of what he was seeing.

"Who are those two?" asked Yuka as everyone shifted their eyes to the two figures that were still coming into focus.

"I don't know," said Daniel. "The next two Demon Lords?"

"Guys, who is that?" asked Yuka as she pointed to a massive, hulking figure that started to appear before the four shadowy figures. He was elevated, sitting on a large stone throne. Behind him was a large window. It was night. In the distance was the peak of a mountain.

Everyone's eyes fixated on the large hulk as Daniel uttered, "That's gotta be the Warlock."

"Guys!" screamed Clara as she pointed. "Why is she moving?"

Everyone focused on the *gumiho*, who started to slowly turn towards them, snapping her head in their direction at the last moment. Her eyes beamed at Sung as he gulped. Eyes widened, the warriors pushed off from the stone slab as the *gumiho* started to walk towards them.

"Why is she moving toward us!" Yuka let out in panic.

The *gumiho* suddenly zoomed toward them so they could see her face up close, just as her head burst through the ghastly water. Everyone stumbled backwards in fear as the watery visage of the *gumiho* looked down at them before focusing her eyes on Sung.

Sung felt his heart palpitating furiously as her icy blue eyes met his. She smiled, but her angelic expression morphed nefariously. Her eyes glowed blue and her ravenous hair flowed tantalizingly behind her.

"Holy crap!" Daniel screamed out loud.

Clara frantically kicked back a couple of steps along the ground as she struggled to pull off her bow from a seated position.

Sung felt his heart drop as he stared back at the cold but seductive face of Jisoo. He gulped as he spotted the Claw Staff lying on the stone slab. A sudden deep resentment welled up from deep within him. He gritted his teeth, lunged forward, and grabbed at the Claw Staff as the glowing blue jade reflected in his eyes, swinging it fast and hard through the watery image. The eerie visage dissolved as droplets of water splashed back into the Origins Pool.

Panting and heart pounding, Sung stepped backwards toward his paralyzed friends as everyone stared at the Origins Pool.

"What did we just do?" asked a terrified Yuka.

TWELVE

Early the next morning, Clara, Sung, Yuka, and Daniel gathered at the Portal Circle. Their nerves were still frayed from the previous night. When their senses returned after their mysterious encounter with the *gumiho*, they raced away from the Origins Pool. Still in shock and a safe distance from the pool, everyone had agreed to meet at the Portal Circle before breakfast.

Sung was still and pensive as Daniel paced in place. Clara was shivering, still reeling from the unexpected summoning. Yuka kept looking around her as if they were going to be found out by the guardians.

"Guys," whispered Clara, but no one looked up. Annoyed, she raised her voice, "Guys!"

Everyone looked up with worried expressions.

"What are we going to do?" asked Yuka and frantically followed up with, "You don't think we brought the *kitsune*, I mean *gumiho*, back into Azen, do you?"

"I don't know," said Daniel.

"This wouldn't have happened if it wasn't for your dumb idea!" stammered Sung as he stared at Daniel.

"I didn't think it would work!" said Daniel defensively. "I was only playing!"

"Guys!" said Clara sternly. "What's done is done. What do we tell the guardians?"

"No way," said Daniel. "You saw how mad the Guardian Buffalo got at me."

"Guardian Tiger will claw me out if he found out," said Sung fearfully.

"I don't want to disappoint my Guardian Crane," pleaded Yuka.

Clara thought to herself that she didn't want to upset her Guardian Panda and wanted to believe that the summoning of the *gumiho* was not that big of a deal. She looked at everyone and said, "Okay, we don't tell our guardians, but we need to be on guard. We carry our weapons everywhere with us, and if the *gumiho* appears, we run and get help. Agreed?"

Everyone nodded in agreement, though the worry in the pit of their stomachs continued gnawing at them.

"Let's think like warriors for a second," said Clara sternly as she looked about her. "So we saw into the Warlock's fortress, and for the first time, we finally saw him. We also know that there are two other Demon Lords. I think we can agree that they will be leading the next two battles. Did anyone see anything else?"

"It was too blurry," said Daniel.

"The mountain peak," Yuka interjected.

"Right," said Clara. "I remember the mountain peak too. What are you doing?"

Daniel was on his tippy toes as she tried to scan over the horizon. He settled back onto his soles and looked at Clara. "I wanted to see if I could see the mountain peak from here."

Clara looked frustrated. "We don't need to do that. We have the Portal Books."

Clara walked over to Yuka's Portal Book as she followed.

"Yuka, since it was the cranes that last saw the fortress before they disappeared, it's got to be in your book," said Clara.

"Right," said Yuka. "So what do you want me to do?"

"Can you weave out the maps similar to how our guardians do it?" asked Clara.

Yuka looked confused as she looked down at the Portal Book. "I can try."

Everyone stood back from Yuka as she placed her right hand onto her Portal Book. Her eyes closed as she willed in her mind the terrain of Azen. In a fluid motion, she arced her hand toward the center of the Portal Circle. Her Portal Book sent up fiery flames as they streamed forth, weaving the terrain of Azen.

Everyone was in awe, and Yuka was gleeful at her success.

Clara spotted the Portal Circle and looking around, easily found the Panda Kingdom to the east, the Tiger Kingdom in the west, the Buffalo Kingdom to the north, and finally the Red Crown Crane Kingdom to the south. But something else caught Clara's attention as she pointed at them.

"Guys," Clara said. "What are those?"

Everyone turned their attention to what seemed like other animal kingdoms throughout Azen.

"Other animal kingdoms?" asked Sung.

"That's got to be the dragon kingdom," said Yuka excitedly. "So cool!"

"And those most be other ones," said Daniel. "I wonder what animals are in those kingdoms?"

"Yah, it's too small to make out anything," said Clara. "Those kingdoms must support the metal warrior."

"Must be," said Sung as he looked at Clara and she looked back at him with a grin.

"Guys," interjected Daniel. "So we know the Warlock is in the east, and I can't see beyond The Shards. Our guardians were right, though. Look at all the chasms. It's impossible to cross by land."

"Oh!" said Yuka with lit eyes as she placed her hand back onto her Portal Book. "I need to summon up Nadi."

Yuka thought for a moment and flung out more streams of fire that assembled the missing part of the terrain at the eastern edge of The Shards: Nadi.

Daniel's eyes lit up as he walked harmlessly through the fiery terrain. "There it is!"

Everyone gathered around Daniel to see what he was looking at. The Warlock's fortress was formidable, a seemingly massive stone fortress jutting out of the mountain itself. Daniel looked eastward and located the mountain peak from the watery image they'd seen the night before. He glanced back toward the fiery representation of the Portal Circle and estimated the distance in his mind.

"So there is his fortress," said Daniel. "Hey Yuka, how fast can you fly?"

"Very fast," said Yuka before her eyes widened with realization. "NO! We are not going there!"

"Chill!" said Daniel as he put up his hands defensively. "I was just wondering."

"Guys!" said Sung urgently. "Someone is coming."

Yuka frantically waved at the streams of fire, blowing at them to put them out. In desperation, she finally shooed at the fiery streams, which flowed back into her Portal Book. Everyone rushed to their Portal Books and started to manifest just as the Guardian Buffalo emerged.

"Emperor and empress warriors," said the Guardian Buffalo as his hooves clattered onto the stone Portal Circle.

Daniel spun around, bowed and uttered, "Good morning, Guardian Buffalo. How did you sleep last night?"

The other emperor and empress warriors turned and bowed, and the Guardian Buffalo reciprocated.

"I slept well," said the Guardian Buffalo. "A quiet night. I hope you all had one too."

Daniel nodded profusely, "Yes, Guardian Buffalo, we all had a quiet night as well."

"That's good," said the Guardian Buffalo. "Shall we head to breakfast? I'm hungry."

Everyone nodded and followed the Guardian Buffalo down the path to the meal table.

* * *

Later that night, after a full day of training, Daniel quietly folded back the flap of his tent quarters and peeked out. He spied a buffalo guard passing by and waited until he was out of sight. With his club horn in hand, he snuck out of the tent encampment and made his way to the Portal Circle. He looked around and saw no one. He checked his training attire and inserted his club horn into the leather sheath across his back.

"Where do you think you're going?" Yuka asked from above.

Daniel's eyes lit up as he looked about and realized his oversight. Yuka had been following him by air and was now floating down to the ground. She landed softly in front of him with her arms crossed in a disapproving expression.

Daniel looked evasive as he replied, "I'm just going to take a joy ride."

"No, you're not," Yuka retorted. "You're going to the Warlock's fortress!"

"Hey, not so loud," said Daniel alarmingly.

"Don't go, Daniel," pleaded Yuka. "It's not safe!"

"Look, it'll be okay," said Daniel. "I just think we need to take some calculated risks. The more information we can get, the more useful we'll be to our armies."

"Daniel," Yuka said sternly. "You mustn't go and defy your Guardian Buffalo's wishes! Remember what happened when Clara and I took an innocent flight?"

"Look, Yuka," said Daniel. "Guardian Buffalo has done so much for me. He made me realize who I am and helped me to embrace my Vietnamese heritage. And now, I realize how much my mother loves me. I'm eternally grateful to him. So if I can do something to help all of us, I will. For whatever reason the cranes failed, I'm sure I won't. We are the Azen Warriors."

"Daniel," Yuka said with more deliberateness. "I'll tell on you if you…"

"I need to go," Daniel interrupted as he invoked the thrust Qi element and soared off into the night sky.

"No!" yelled Yuka with frustration. As she looked up, she could see Daniel's fiery thrust growing dimmer. Her hands fanned out across her Moon Star as five additional stars replicated on each side of her waist. She angrily brushed the *fly* Qi element into the air as she blurted out, "*tobu!*" She soared off into the night sky after Daniel.

THIRTEEN

Yuka caught up with Daniel and continued to plead, but he dismissed her concerns. She tried to shove him out of the air, but his aerial skills were on par with hers and he evaded them. Finally, she gave up convincing him to turn around. She regretted not acting on her suspicions and telling the Guardian Crane of Daniel's desire to see the Warlock's fortress himself. She could have also told Clara, but she didn't. Without telling anyone, she realized that no one knew where they were, but she couldn't leave Daniel alone on his reckless journey.

"Yuka!" screamed Daniel. But Yuka ignored him. She felt obliged to fly with Daniel to keep an eye on him, but she didn't have to give him the satisfaction of acknowledging him.

When she didn't answer for the fifth time, Daniel knew she was mad at him, but he brushed aside her concerns. *The risk was low,* he thought, *and besides, all he wanted to do was look around. Where had there ever been any harm in just looking around?*

They had been flying east for about an hour, and he looked down at the glassy barren land below. The Guardian Buffalo was right. The entire terrain was like jagged obsidian glass, with long, wide, and deep chasms carved into its glistening surface. The eerie silence was deafening. Daniel invoked another thrust Qi element and clenched his fist harder. He flew ahead of Yuka.

Yuka could see the fiery thrust around his ankles. Unlike his thrust, which could be seen as the air ruffled behind him, her flight was stealthy. She invoked another Qi element herself and clenched hard as she raced through the air. She came up onto this right side and pulled ahead of him by one body length. When he turned to her, she ignored him. She knew she was faster as she was the most natural flyer between them.

They continued to fly in tense silence. When he tried to pull ahead of her, she easily pulled ahead of him, proving her prowess of flight.

As they neared three hours of flying time, Yuka started to see a change in the terrain: trees. It started out sparsely, a dark tree here and there, then clumps until finally they were over a dark forest.

"Hey," hollered Daniel as he looked at Yuka.

She looked over at him with annoyance. He looked at her and then ahead while pointing. Yuka looked in his direction and saw it: A lone mountain peak, but in the foreground, some distance off, a mammoth structure stood out from another jagged mountainside: the Warlock's fortress.

It jutted high up out of the mountain, where strangely, there were trees along a seemingly rocky mountainside. Soft glowing lights emanated from windows along its stone walls. As they neared it, Yuka felt a sense of nervousness and curiosity. They were close, and Yuka turned to Daniel, who was looking at her. She turned her gaze toward his feet and was alarmed by his fiery thrust.

"They'll see you!" she hollered.

Daniel nodded and scanned the forest until his eyes spotted a clearing on a mountain plateau below the fortress. He pointed down to it, and Yuka nodded. They started to descend into the treetops. Both Yuka and Daniel floated down, feet first. Though both were silent on their descent, Yuka looked nervously at his fiery feet, which extinguished themselves before he landed with a thud. Yuka floated down and touched the ground silently.

"See, that wasn't so bad," said Daniel cajolingly.

"Hmph," uttered Yuka as she took a couple of steps and looked up. The dark sky above, illuminated slightly by the moonlight, was obscured by sprawling and gnarly branches. "These trees..."

Daniel took a couple of steps forward as he tried to peer between the tree branches. "What about them?" he asked."

"They don't have any leaves," said Yuka.

"Maybe it's fall," said Daniel. "Hey, there. Look!"

Yuka came up alongside him as he pointed into the distance. She looked and saw it as well. Several dim amber lights fluttered from the windows in the fortress.

"There it is," said Daniel in a hushed tone as Yuka nodded.

Daniel scanned the numerous dark and gnarly trees up ahead and started to walk forward. He turned back toward Yuka and whispered, "Come on."

Yuka looked around and followed him as a branch above her gently swayed in the calm night.

They meandered amongst the trees, moving about as quietly as possible through the underbrush. Yuka noticed that the rocky terrain seemed lifeless. She looked about often, remembering her harrowing experience with the *Huo Dou* demon dogs on that fateful night when she went to rescue Clara beyond Jagged Pass. She was expecting glowing eyes of a pack of demon dogs to rush them or a couple of *nues* would suddenly appear from above with their snapping snake tails. After what seemed like half an hour, the trees started to open up, and they could see the dark stone structure of the Warlock's fortress high above.

Yuka came up on Daniel's right as she stared up at the fortress. It was L-shaped with the longer wing near them while the shorter wing rested on a mountainous ledge. It was several stories tall with glowing light emanating from the evenly spaced-out windows on its upper half. The roof over the longer part of the structure was pitched, while the roof on the other part of the building seemed to glisten. A long, stone ramp ran uphill towards an arched entrance with a menacing gate. The archway was aglow from large, fiery torches. It was eerily silent.

"This place is giving me the shivers," said Yuka.

Daniel took a few steps forward as Yuka suddenly reached out and pleaded, "Don't go too far."

Daniel turned around as the moon beams rained down on this left cheek, highlighting his face.

"Daniel! Behind you!" screamed Yuka as her eyes bulged.

Daniel spun around in alarm to see a swarm of branches closing in on him. Before he could react, a strong gust of wind ripped through the branches, snapping them into pieces. An ear-wrenching howl filled the air as Daniel turned toward Yuka, with her hand stretched outward. But his eyes trained on the dark, moving trees as fiery yellowish eyes and mouths appeared on their trunks. They propelled themselves along the ground with their roots as their sinewy branches reached out for Yuka.

Daniel invoked a fireball and aimed it at one of the trees, setting it ablaze and pushing it back, and then he sent another. The trees with the sinister faces surrounded them as Yuka frantically sent up another gust of wind that barreled into another tree. Another stronger gust to her right sent a couple of trees backward.

"They're after us!" screamed Yuka as a fire burst exploded upon another tree on her left.

"We need to get out now!" screamed Daniel as he invoked another fireball that exploded against another tree. But to his horror, the trees absorbed his fire as their smiles became more sinister.

The branches of the trees started to tangle into a mesh above them. With all her might, Yuka sent up the strongest gust of wind that she could muster, snapping the tree branches as a crescendo of howls was released.

Daniel saw his opportunity and thrusted through the hole that Yuka created. "Come on, Yuka!" he screamed.

Yuka flew upward when suddenly, something grabbed her ankles. Yuka screamed as the branches dragged her down, and as she tried to invoke another gust, slender branches raced along her right arm to her fingers and immobilized them as she watched in horror.

"No!" screamed Yuka as she looked up to see the opening in the sky filling ominously with branches. Another fireball flew towards them, but to no effect as more branches took their place. Tendrils of branches snaked over her left arm and thicker branches encircled her waist, pulling her downward. "Help me!" were the last words she managed to utter as the tree pulled her against its trunk, nearly smothering her. Fear gripped her as soft slimy branches spread over mouth.

Meanwhile, Daniel hovered above, frantically throwing down the strongest fireballs that he could muster. But despite their cataclysmic explosions, the trees seemed to be absorbing his fire. Daniel hovered in despair as the entire forest writhed grotesquely.

"YUKA!" he screamed as beads of sweat slid down his temples. His breathing raced as he saw a tree break the tree line and race toward the ramp. *Yuka!* He was about to fly toward the tree when several packs of fire demon dogs raced out of the gate, barking loudly. He looked down again in desperation and suddenly saw many trees following the first one, giving it cover as the fire demon dogs raced past them.

Daniel hovered in the air helplessly. His face crumbling in emotion, he yelled out one more time, "Yuka!"

He clenched his fists, looking up at the fire bursts being launched at him by the packs of the fiery demon dogs. "Damn it!" he yelled as he dodged the fire bursts.

He pivoted in the air and thrust back toward Azen, leaving Yuka behind.

FOURTEEN

"Empress Warrior Wu!" yelled the Guardian Panda, rushing into her tent quarters.

Startled awake, Clara jolted from her bed.

The Guardian Panda's face was illuminated by his jade torch as he said urgently, "Empress Warrior Wu!"

Clara turned to him as she wiped her sleepy eyes, "What? I'm up."

"Please get changed and follow me."

Clara looked up at his startled expression, "What's going on? What happened?" as she turned over the covers.

The Guardian Panda looked down at Clara gravely with his worried brown eyes, "Empress Warrior Satoh has been captured."

Clara followed the Guardian Panda out of the tent in a hurry with her bow and quiver across her body. Clara was still adjusting the outer edge of her training top. She had never seen the Guardian Panda so agitated.

"What happened?" asked Clara as her thoughts went to Yuka.

"Carelessness," mumbled the Guardian Panda.

As they neared the Portal Circle, she could hear someone yelling. She looked up and saw Sung frantically waving his hands at Daniel. The other guardians were there as several panda, tiger, buffalo, and crane attendants stood on the outer perimeter of the Portal Circle.

"How could you!" Sung was yelling at Daniel, who was an emotional wreak, just as Clara arrived.

The Guardian Buffalo looked up at Clara and said in a stern voice, "Emperor Warrior Nguyen and Empress Warrior Satoh flew to the Warlock's fortress earlier tonight."

Clara glared at Daniel. "What?! You said you were just joking about going there after you convinced Sung to summon the *gumiho* from the Origins Pool!"

All the guardians' ears and eyes perked up as Daniel stammered with a trembling voice, "We were just curious! We thought we'd fly there, take a look around, and then fly back."

"Liar!" screamed Clara. "It was your idea, right?"

Daniel looked up remorsefully at Clara as she stepped toward him when the Guardian Buffalo interjected.

"What is this about the *gumiho* and the Origins Pool?" he asked.

Clara turned to the Guardian Buffalo and she realized that their little secret was out. Guilt and embarrassment started to entangle themselves in the pit of her stomach. Her anger lent to their confession. "We were at the Origins Pool the other night and Daniel convinced Sung to summon…"

"It's not like I forced him to!" Daniel blurted out.

Her slap spun Daniel's head to the right, where it stayed as Clara raised her hand once more but Sung grabbed her wrist.

Her eyes were red with fury as she stared back at Sung's pleading eyes. She ripped her hand out of Sung's grip and stared at Daniel, whose head spun back around as he choked back on his emotions.

"You're reckless! You're undisciplined! You're pig-headed. This is the part of you that is not Asian!" screamed Clara as her voice reached a crescendo.

"It's all my fault," uttered Daniel remorsefully as he crumbled to the ground with his face in his hands.

"Empress Warrior Wu, Emperor Warrior Kim, and Nguyen," said the Guardian Tiger as he stepped in. "We need you to put aside your emotions and think about Empress Warrior Satoh's life right now. Emperor Warrior Nguyen, stand!"

Daniel straightened up and wiped away his tears without looking at anyone.

The Guardian Panda and the Crane stepped in closer as the Guardian Tiger asked, "Emperor Warrior Kim, tell us more about how you summoned the *gumiho*."

Sung exhaled and he told them just as he had summoned his own parents, he summoned the *gumiho* in the same way. Only this time, he thought about her and called out her name in his mind: Jisoo. He retold how the ghostly image appeared in the water, and how they could make out the Warlock and his four Demon Lords in the fortress. He went on with how everyone was surprised that the *gumiho* turned around and burst out of the water, staring down at them. He ended the haunting watery visage by slicing through it with the Claw Staff.

"This has never happened before," said the puzzled Guardian Tiger.

"I was joking that since she inhaled his Qi, maybe some strange connection was created," Daniel uttered as he looked up slightly. "But I didn't think it would work!"

"No matter how it happened," said the Guardian Buffalo. "It seems that by summoning her here, she was able to sense Daniel's desire to see the fortress for himself. They were expecting you."

"Damn it!" Daniel cried out when he realized his mistake.

"Emperor Warrior Nguyen," said the Guardian Buffalo. "Control yourself."

"What are we going to do?" asked the Guardian Panda.

"Rescue her," said the Guardian Crane whose voice carried a deep hint of sorrow. As all eyes turned onto her she said gravely, "We need to rescue Empress Warrior Satoh. It is my sworn duty."

"I'll go," Daniel volunteered as he looked up with his bloodshot teary eyes.

"Haven't you already done enough?" scolded Clara.

"Enough!" the Guardian Crane shrieked.

Silence fell over the group causing the attendants outside of the Portal Circle to take a step back.

"Time is not on our side," said the Guardian Crane curtly. "We need to mount a rescue now while the Warlock least expects it. The Top Talon team and I will rescue Yuka. We'll need the Prowlers for this mission."

"You will have them," said the Guardian Tiger.

"Thank you," said the Guardian Crane as she looked at Clara. "And I will need you, Empress Warrior Wu, to be part of this mission."

Clara looked to the Guardian Panda as Sung and Daniel looked at her, "But the pandas, they'll be powerless."

"The Warlock is after her Qi, and we may need you to restore it before it is too late," explained the Guardian Crane sadly.

Clara nodded in understanding, "Of course."

"Then I'm coming too," said the Guardian Panda as the Guardian Crane looked at him with her beady eyes. "I'm sworn to protect Empress Warrior Wu."

The Guardian Crane's eyes blinked, and she nodded in understanding. She looked around at everyone but settled her last glance on the warriors.

"This unfortunate incident is also happening at the worst time," explained the Guardian Crane. "This next lunar eclipse is happening in a few moments. If the next battle is to the south, we have ample time to prepare. But if it is to the north, we only have half a day to reach it.

"The battle vessels of the Buffalo Kingdom are already deployed should the next battle be to the north. We can hold them off until your arrival." said the Guardian Buffalo.

"This next battle, it could happen in the afternoon?" asked Sung.

The Guardian Crane nodded. "Yes, that is a possibility, Emperor Warrior Kim. Until we bring back Empress Warrior Satoh safely along with Empress Warrior Wu, the armor of the crane and panda armies will not be powered. When the jades of the Moon Star *shuriken* and the Bow of Destiny cross over The Shards or water, all like jades are rendered powerless. It has always been that way. They will only be protected by their armor. You and Emperor Warrior Nguyen will be battling the third Warlock army alone."

Sung gulped as Daniel stood frozen as the daunting reality of their challenge sunk in. Without a moment's notice, their eyes dimmed as they looked up.

Everyone looked up as a pall settled onto the Portal Circle. "The third lunar eclipse is starting," said the Guardian Crane as her tone dipped. "We call this one, *zhēnzhū*."

Clara recognized the Mandarin word for *pearl* and looked up. The pearly moon started to move into the earth's shadow. But the doom it portended seemed different at that moment. Darkness soon descended upon the Portal Circle as the glowing eyes of the guardians stood out eerily in the dark. Soon enough, the moon started to creep out of the earth's shadow until it continued its high arc into the sky.

The Guardian Crane dipped her beak down and lowered her gaze to everyone and simply said, "We need to rescue Empress Warrior Satoh."

FIFTEEN

The snarly brownish-yellowish roots of the *Xuong Cuong* howling demon tree rippled smoothly and silently along the stone slab floor of the Warlock's throne room. Its branches held Yuka taut against its trunk as they wrapped around her torso. Branches clamped down her legs, holding them firmly in place as sinewy branches slithered down her arms while tendrils of branches held her fingers in place, preventing Yuka from invoking her Qi elemental powers. Sinewy branches slithered over her mouth, leaving only Yuka's frightened eyes visible as her nostrils flared in fear.

As the tree approached, followed by two other trees and a pack of demon dogs, the massive Warlock rose from his throne with excitement on his face. The four Demon Lords also turned to see the tree that stopped just before the throne.

"Never in all my years," the Warlock hollered incredulously as he stepped down from the stone throne, "did I think that a warrior of Azen would ever be in my presence! What a fortuitous omen!"

Yuka uttered a few muffled sounds as the Warlock lumbered into view and stared at her.

"How foolish that you came to my fortress," taunted the Warlock. "But how fortunate your foolishness was for me!"

The Warlock gave a hearty laugh of satisfaction that echoed throughout the throne room as the four Demon Lords came up to each side of him to glare at his helpless prize.

The Warlock's yellowish-black eyes glided over Yuka's frame. With a wave of his hand, the branches along her torso pulled away, revealing her rumpled training top and the Moon Star *shuriken*. The white jade glistened, and the Warlock's eyes lit up. His large leathery skinned index finger pressed up hard against Yuka's chest as she winced at the pressure on her chest. Her breathing hastened as he slid this index finger down onto her softer belly. Yuka's eyes bulged and she let out a painful gasp as his finger pressed into her belly. He watched her reaction with curiosity.

"How can something so weak be so powerful?" questioned the Warlock as he stared into Yuka's frightened eyes. Finally, his finger came upon the Moon Star, which he plucked from her waist. Yuka looked defeated as she stared at her Moon Star in between the Warlock's thumb and index finger as he coveted it.

The *gumiho* walked gracefully over to the Warlock as he marveled at the Moon Star. Yuka's eyes looked into the sinister but seductive eyes of the *gumiho* as her nine fluffy white tails ruffled gently behind her. She came in close and angled her nose under Yuka's chin and inhaled. She pulled back in delight as she gently ran her fingertip down Yuka's chest and stopped at her heart. She poked hard, causing Yuka to squirm and wince. Then she pulled her delicate finger away.

"Her Qi is strong," said Jisoo. "I can sense it. It would be such a pleasure to siphon her."

The Warlock looked down at the *gumiho* and saw her unsatiable appetite for Yuka's Qi.

"Put your finger down," said the Warlock. Jisoo cowered a bit and obeyed as her nine fluffy tails drooped slightly in disappointment.

The Warlock stepped in front of Yuka and exhaled. With an upward wave of his hand, the roots of the tree pushed upward, raising Yuka to the level of the Warlock's menacing face. The Warlock looked at her and spoke.

"We know now that we can render the jade's power useless by shattering what we thought was once unbreakable. We also know that you, my loyal nine-tailed Demon Lord, can siphon off their Qi, bringing a hollow death to these wretched warriors of Azen. Though the male warriors would be better for your appetite. Yet, that would do me no good. Perhaps we can extract the Qi through more conventional methods."

A slender demon tree slithered across the stone floor and stopped next to the tree holding Yuka. Its eyes looked at the Warlock in a reverent manner before he asked, "Yes my Lord, how would you like me to proceed?"

The Warlock looked over Yuka's body once more before looking at the second tree.

"Use those branches of yours, Harvester, and find a way to extract her Qi. Keep me updated on your progress at every hour," said the Warlock callously as he stared once more into Yuka's terrified eyes.

"As you wish," said the Harvester tree as the first tree lowered itself, turned around, and rippled away from the Warlock as Yuka's muffled pleas faded.

SIXTEEN

At the Portal Circle, everyone scattered in different directions. Sung and a shaken Daniel left with their respective guardians to reassess their defenses.

Clara's mind was in a frenzy as she thought about the potentially horrible things that may be happening to Yuka. A vision of the nine-tailed fox siphoning her Qi caused her heart to skip a beat when the Guardian Panda interrupted her morbid thoughts.

"Empress Warrior Wu," whispered the Guardian Panda.

Clara looked up as they slowed their brisk walk, "Yes, Guardian Panda?"

"When you reach your tent, wait for the attendants to help you get into your battle armor," he said gravely.

Clara nodded as she contemplated the weight of the situation.

"Once you suit up, meet me back at the Portal Circle," the Guardian Panda said as he started to leave toward his tent.

Clara nodded as she hurried off to her tent, clutching the Bow of Destiny and feeling the reassurance of the Bamboo Jade underneath it. She burst into the tent, slipped out of her shoes, unslung the bow and quiver as she placed them onto the bed. When the tent flap opened, she spun around with her heart racing. Three panda attendants entered, wheeling in another wardrobe.

Clara's eyes lit up in curiosity as the wardrobe was tilted upright short of her bed. The two panda attendants each grabbed a door and opened it as Clara's eyes lit up.

"Whoa," said Clara.

Clara's eyes glided over the blackened battle armor before her. It was similar to her familiar battle armor, but it was more contoured to her body. The black was matte, absorbing the ambient light. One of the panda attendants passed by her as the other panda attendant was met by the panda attendant from behind the wardrobe.

One of the attendants spoke, "Empress Warrior Wu, this is your blackout armor, used for stealth missions. We are here to get you into it."

Clara nodded as she began removing her training attire. The panda attendants helped Clara slip into a black mesh body suit. A stretchable gaiter mask was slipped over and around her neck. The contoured chest plate magnetically fit over her torso. The shoulder guards along with the integrated neck guard clipped into place. The waist armor was strapped on. Thigh guards and forearm gauntlets magnetically latched onto the mesh bodysuit. She slipped into her blackened boots as each heel slipped into place with a thud. Her regular quiver was replaced with a blackened quiver along with a set of black-coated jade-tipped arrows.

"How come the arrow tips are black?" asked Clara.

"They've been dipped in onyx powder," one of the panda attendants responded.

"What is that?" asked Clara as she slung the quiver across her back.

"It is a special powder here on Azen derived from the natural decay of the illumination jades. Once an illumination jade is exposed to light for the first time; its life of illumination begins. But the light of the illumination jades is not infinite and will decay anywhere from ninety to one hundred years. Once its light is dimmed, the entire jade decays into this powder, which we call onyx powder. We have found that it will adhere to any surface and absorb all light before it starts to fall off in about six hours. It is what we are now applying to your bow," said the panda attendant as she looked at the other panda attendant. "Begin now."

Clara watched the other panda as he nodded. He gently placed the Bow of Destiny onto the rack and flipped open a bamboo container. He gently shook out a fine black powder over the length of the bow. Each black particle automatically clung to the bow and soon, the entire Bow of Destiny was covered in black. The panda attendant then extended the blacked-out Bow of Destiny toward Clara, who took it in both hands.

As her eyes looked at it, she softly let out, "Cool! But…"

"Yes, Empress Warrior Wu?" asked the panda attendant.

"When I cross into Nadi, will the Bamboo Jade help with the aim?" asked Clara.

The panda attendant blinked and responded, "I cannot answer that for you, Empress Warrior Wu. To my knowledge, no warrior of Azen has ever crossed into Nadi."

Clara nodded.

"One more item, Empress Warrior Wu," said the panda attendant from behind as Clara spun around as she slung the bow across her chest.

The panda attendant presented a blackened helmet. Clara took it in both of her hands as she looked down at it in awe.

Moments later, the tent flapped opened as Clara stepped out into the cool night in her blackout armor. She loved how the armor felt and how it transformed her. She exhaled and placed her palm over the blacked-out Bamboo Jade.

"Good luck, Empress Warrior Wu," said one of the three pandas at the tent entrance.

Clara turned back to them, nodded and replied, "We'll get her back."

Clara briskly walked toward the Portal Circle. She was the first to arrive. She exhaled into the cool night and looked around her. All was silent. The four Portal Books were all gently glowing. She walked over to her Portal Book and stared down at it when she felt a soft wind behind her. Clara turned around but didn't see anything when suddenly, two beady eyes blinked at her. Clara instinctively took a step back as a familiar voice said, "Empress Warrior Wu, it is I, the Guardian Crane."

Clara squinted and soon, with the help of the moonbeams, she could make out the shadowy silhouette of the large Guardian Crane and four additional cranes behind her.

"Whoa, I can barely see you!" exclaimed Clara.

"Then I know it's working," said the Guardian Crane as she outstretched her wings and Clara could make out the *katana* wings, which were also blacked out.

"What's working?" asked Clara.

"The onyx powder," said the Guardian Crane. "We've all been dusted in it to give us maximum stealth advantage."

"Whoa," said Clara as she blinked. "There are only five cranes?"

"Yes," said the Guardian Crane. "The rescue team needs to be small and nimble, but we will have help."

"We have arrived," said the Guardian Tiger as he sauntered up along with three pairs of glowing eyes behind him.

Clara squinted and she could make out the muscular and sleek shapes of three blacked-out tigers. They were menacing shadows sauntering through the night.

"I have arrived as well," said the familiar voice of the Guardian Panda.

Clara spun around and couldn't see the Guardian Panda.

"Over here, Empress Warrior Wu," said the Guardian Panda's voice.

Clara followed the sound of his voice until two barely noticeable brown eyes stared back at her, then finally, the familiar outline of the Guardian Panda came into view. All his white fur was black, and he was squeezed into a blacked-out mesh body suit. Across his chest was his blacked-out bow and quiver along his back.

"Wow, I can barely see you," said Clara.

The Guardian Panda responded, "Yes, the onyx powder is working."

"The final team members are approaching," said the Guardian Crane as Clara turned around to hear the rustling of wings. Clara looked all about until a tiny pair of eyes hovered in front of her. Curiously, Clara twisted her head until she could see a tiny, blacked-out bird in front of her face. She raised her hand, and the bird rested on it as she smiled at how adorable it was.

"This is Michi, leader of our scout squadron," said the Guardian Crane. "She and her team gather intel on our enemy."

As Clara fawned over Michi, she spoke in a soft voice, "It is an honor to meet you, Empress Warrior Wu. It may be hard to see now, but my squadron is fifty strong. Squadron, please chirp so we can hear you."

A chorus of chirps broke the silence, and Clara looked up to see numerous tiny blinking eyes above the other blacked-out cranes.

"I am honored to meet you," said Clara.

"We will get Empress Warrior Satoh back," said Michi as she flew off and settled onto one of the blacked-out cranes.

The Guardian Crane circled around quickly and eyed the four blacked-out cranes, three tigers, the Guardian Panda, Clara, and the Guardian Tiger, in his full white-and-black striped glory, who was staying behind.

"Fellow warriors," said the Guardian Crane. "Time is of the essence. At the Top Talon's top speed, we should be at the Warlock's fortress in about two hours. We have only one mission: to rescue Empress Warrior Satoh from the clutches of the Warlock and his Demon Lords. Everything else is irrelevant. The scouts will find a way in, and once Empress Warrior Satoh is located, we shall get her. Remember, your armor is not protected by the jade, since it is inert over The Shards. We do not know if the jade will power up once we cross into Nadi. Once we cross into Nadi, Empress Warrior Wu, please power up your jade and we shall see if the Bamboo Jade will power up. Also, Empress Warrior Wu, your earth Qi may not be effective as you will not be standing on earth in his mountainous fortress, though your restorative Qi will work from one warrior to another. Let's hope that it will not come to that. We have had the advantage of the warrior's jade, but for this rescue, we must rely on our training. Are there any questions?"

There was a pause before the Guardian Tiger emitted a low growl. "The fire signal in the north was lit, the Warlock's army has been transported there. We'll hold the battle in the north and leave you some fight upon your return with Empress Warrior Satoh."

The Guardian Crane nodded, "We shall."

The Guardian Tiger looked at the blacked-out Guardian Panda, "Be careful, old friend."

The Guardian Panda looked over with his soulful eyes and said, "Always, old friend."

"Let's mount up. Scouts on your designated cranes. Prowlers, to your cranes. Guardian Panda, Shiori will take you. And Clara," said the Guardian Crane.

"Yes?" asked Clara.

"You're with me," said the Guardian Crane as she lowered herself.

Clara exhaled and bit her lip. After fumbling with her hands to find the contour of the blacked-out Guardian Crane's body, she climbed onto her back.

As the four cranes stepped into formation behind the Guardian Crane and Clara harnessed herself in, the Guardian Crane addressed her cranes.

"Top Talon team," said the Guardian Crane with authority as she said *ascend* in Japanese, "*jōshō suru!*"

The Guardian Tiger watched as the Top Talon cranes flapped into the air. His eyesight was unparalleled but soon, the night swallowed up the team of blacked-out cranes as they flew in determination to rescue Empress Warrior Satoh.

SEVENTEEN

Yuka's muffled screams of pain somehow slipped through the branches covering her mouth, and her eyes rolled back in agony, tears seeping from their corners. As two tendrils of branches withdrew from her face, her nostrils flared as she gulped in precious air and choked back the cries lodged in her throat.

Her body relaxed against the burly branches holding her firmly in place on the cold stone examination table. Channels for draining blood ran lengthwise along the edges and converged at the end into a spout, where a stone crucible would collect the dripping blood. Thankfully, it was empty at the moment.

The captor demon tree was at the head of the stone examination table, extending all its branches to hold Yuka in place. The strongest of its branches held down Yuka's torso. A slithery pair ran down her arms while skinny tendrils wrapped around Yuka's fingers, preventing her from invoking her Qi elemental powers. Another set of branches stretched firmly over her legs, and a pair of fresh branches muffled her mouth, keeping her from yelling out any of her Qi elemental commands. The Captor's glowing yellowish eyes and mouth pulsated as it looked down at its hostage.

The Harvester was probing methodically for a way to extract the Qi from Yuka's body. It had never extracted Qi from a living warrior before, but that didn't stop it from taking pleasure in his efforts. The slender tendrils that had just explored Yuka's nostrils glistened. It brought them closer to its glowing eyes. After examining its probing tendrils, it blinked and whipped its branch with such force that the tips of the probing tendrils snapped off. The two broken tendrils bounced onto the floor along with other discarded tendrils, which shriveled up.

The Harvester beamed at Yuka as her eyes pleaded for him to stop. Her muffled pain gave it pleasure. The tree sprouted two new tendrils from its branch as Yuka, in a final attempt to free herself, tensed up against the sturdy branches holding her down. But her efforts were to no avail. Her strength was drained as her body collapsed beneath the branches.

The Harvester was moving in once again with a fresh pair of probing tendrils when heavy thudding footsteps caught his attention. The Harvester pulled back as two large demon dogs entered, followed by the Warlock. He looked down at his two demon dogs, who sat obediently on their haunches at each side of the entrance.

The Warlock looked impatient as he stepped toward the stone table, where Yuka stared back at him trembling. He came around the opposite side of the table facing the Harvester.

"Well?" he asked in a low voice as he beamed at the Harvester.

"Nothing yet, my Lord," said the Harvester as it retracted its top branches into a respectful array that crackled slightly. "It's only been a few hours. It was necessary to get a sense of how her Qi traverses her frail body before I probe this warrior and determine a way to extract it."

"I don't care for your want of anatomical curiosity," the Warlock's voice thundered as the Harvester and the captor tree shuddered. "All I want is her Qi transferred into me!"

The Harvester bowed slightly but entreated, "My Lord, I don't know what I am dealing with here. This is my first time performing an extraction on a live warrior. We should savor... I mean, take our time to examine this opportunity fully."

The Warlock was silent as he glared at the Harvester. He soon turned his ferocious glare at Yuka and waved at her torso. The Warlock stepped up to the table's edge and pressed his palm onto Yuka's chest after the Captor's branches pulled away. Yuka let out a muffled scream as she felt her chest being crushed by the weight of his hand. The Warlock lifted his hand as Yuka inhaled in pain. Then his hand came down upon her chest once more, filling her with crushing pain.

The Warlock took delight in Yuka's cries as she tried desperately to ask for mercy. He relieved the pressure of his palm upon her chest and looked at the Harvester.

"So weak, yet so deceptively strong, these warriors," said the Warlock with disgust.

The Warlock finally lifted his palm from Yuka's chest. She quickly inhaled deeply through her nose and wailed as her eyes shifted away from the Warlock.

With his arms crossed, the Warlock looked sternly at the Harvester, "What is your next... anatomical experiment?"

The Harvester almost smiled in delight as its roots rippled along the floor toward the back counter behind the captor tree. Its glowing yellowish eyes cast down on an assortment of glassware, probes, blades, and assorted metallic instruments in all shapes and sizes. Branches opened wooden drawers until finally it fixated on thick, blackened sheets of paper. The Harvester's eyes glowed as it selected one sheet, a match, a square piece of metal, and a spherical glass cup.

With the four items in its branches, it rippled silently back to the examination table as Yuka's stared, terrified. The Harvester held up all four items for the Warlock to see. The Warlock didn't understand what they were, but he waved brusquely. "Get on with it," he said.

The Harvester looked away from the Warlock and met the gaze of the captor tree. Both of their eyes glowed, silently communicating the next steps. The Harvester struck the match along the stone table and lit the blackened paper, which burst into flames. It dropped the flaming paper into the glass cup.

The captor tree pinched Yuka's nostrils shut with a newly sprouted tendril as the branches covering Yuka's mouth withdrew. Gasping for air, Yuka struggled to scream *gust*: "*Toppū! Toppū!*"

But before she could finish, the spherical glass and flaming paper were abruptly cupped over her mouth. She cringed at the sting of flames upon her lips. But what came next was a pain she'd never experienced as the fire burned off the remaining air within her lungs, collapsing them within her chest. Red veins spiderwebbed themselves along the whites of her eyes as tears gushed. With her last remaining strength, she tensed up every last muscle fiber within her petite body as her vision started to fade to black.

But as the glass was pulled away, her vision returned, blurred from pain-soaked tears. A piece of metal was quickly slipped beneath the glass bottom to hold in the essence from the extraction.

Yuka gasped for air, her chest heaving and lips tingling with fiery pain. She tried again to invoke a Qi elemental power, but the only word she could eke out was, "Help…"

The Harvester looked down at its pathetic captive and looked back up at the captor tree. With a flick of a branch, the ashes from the blackened paper flew from Yuka's lips. The Captor's branch tendrils wove back over Yuka's mouth as she choked helplessly.

The Harvester presented the covered glass to the Warlock, who gazed upon it and looked up dubiously at him.

"She is the air Wu element," said the Harvester. "It is reasonable to presume that her Qi would be carried in her breath, which I have extracted."

The Warlock looked back up at the Harvester curiously. "How do you suggest I ingest her Qi?"

"Inhale it, of course," said the Harvester as it extended the cup toward the Warlock.

The Warlock took the glass cup along with the square piece of metal covering its opening. He looked at it in wonderment. It looked tiny in his large, leathery hands. He glanced at the Harvester, who looked on curiously.

The Warlock brought the cup close to his lips. He slipped off the metal square covering the glass and quickly pressed his lips over the glass to inhale what he had hoped would be Yuka's Qi.

He pulled the glass away and pressed his lips together, ensuring that Yuka's airy essence would not escape. He stayed still for a minute with his eyes closed as the Harvester and captor tree watched in silence.

His eyelids flickered open as his right hand whipped toward the floor, sending the glass cup shattering onto the stone floor.

"Nothing!" hollered the Warlock as he looked menacingly at Yuka's trembling eyes. "Try it again, I may need more!"

The Harvester bowed as Yuka shook her head in fear. The Harvester rippled across the floor and repeated the same painful extraction process, not once, not twice, but five more times until finally, the Warlock violently threw the last glass down onto the floor.

Yuka's energy was drained, her body limp from the pain, her lungs traumatized by the Harvester's torments. She could no longer feel her limbs as a cold she had never felt before started to course through them. Her breaths were shallow, and her reddened eyes could no longer shed any more tears.

"This is a waste of time!" screamed the Warlock as he suddenly growled toward the ceiling. As his gaze settled back onto the repentant Harvester, he demanded, "What other bright ideas do you have for extracting Qi from her puny body?"

The Harvester looked petrified, then suddenly looked up. It bowed beseechingly toward the Warlock as it quickly rippled back toward the counter. Additional branches snaked along the counter as the clanking of glass reverberated, along with the sound of wooden drawers opening and closing. Two long branches unfurled, revealing five glass cups and more blackened paper in each branch. Tendrils along another pair of branches were each holding a match over the blackened paper in each cup.

The Harvester's eyes narrowed deviously, and it spoke. "The air from her lungs is fleeting. Perhaps her Qi is melded into her body, and that is from where it needs to be extracted."

"Intriguing," said the Warlock. "Proceed."

The Harvester tree nodded and turned toward the captor tree. With a flurry of branches, the Captor roughly flipped Yuka onto her stomach. Her body landed with a thud as her head banged onto the stone table. Yuka felt the wind knocked out of her as her head throbbed. The Captor's branches slithered around Yuka's mouth and over her limbs and body, immobilizing her. The captor tree suddenly ripped down the back of her training top, exposing her flawless skin.

"Wait," said the Warlock. "Release the branches from her mouth, ensure she's conscious."

The captor tree's branches along Yuka's mouth slithered away as her hair splayed across her face. A shallow breath was heard, as a whisper slipped from Yuka's mouth, "Please... stop."

The Harvester nodded back at the Warlock. The Warlock crossed his arms and furrowed his brow as he nodded at the Harvester. The Harvester rippled toward the other end of the table. With a single smooth motion, it struck the ten matches against the stone table in unison before dropping them all at once into the ten glass cups as flames flared from the blackened paper.

The Harvester tree then quickly inverted all ten flaming cups along Yuka's spine. Searing pain ripped through Yuka's near-lifeless body as flames flicked against her and sucked her skin into the glass, shooting pain through every muscle.

Yuka's last scream reverberated throughout and beyond the fortress's walls.

EIGHTEEN

Clara pressed hard against the nape of the Guardian Crane. She had always wanted to fly atop the Guardian Crane as Yuka had suggested, but she never felt comfortable asking her. But now, she was flying atop the most graceful and most powerful crane in all of Red-Crowned Crane Kingdom. The best of the Top Talon team had been summoned to rescue Yuka.

Clara's new blackout armor pressed up against the soft blacked-out mesh body suit worn by the Guardian Crane along with the other cranes. The wind rushed along her body as the harness dug into her lower back. She had never seen the cranes fly so fast, but it was necessary to reach Yuka in time to rescue her from the clutches of the Warlock.

The entire flight was silent, and all Clara could do was hold on as her thoughts were consumed with Yuka's safety. She couldn't imagine what Yuka must be going through, all alone at the mercy of the Warlock and his Demon Lords. *Was the nine-tailed fox trying to siphon the Qi from Yuka? What other tortuous ways could they extract her Qi, and was it even possible?* But her thoughts also turned to anger at Daniel. His recklessness and selfishness were what led to Yuka's capture and perhaps endangered the safety of all four kingdoms. All because he was curious and arrogant about his flying capabilities. And when Yuka flew after him, did he think of her? Yuka was the superior flyer, but he should never have put her in that situation. Her fists clenched harder each time she thought of Daniel's poor judgment.

Clara turned her head to the left, where she could barely make out the two blacked-out cranes with the blacked-out tigers riding atop of them. They too were wearing their sleek Clawdium spun battle suits, their fur dusted in onyx powder. She looked to her right, where the last tiger was at the outermost formation while the Guardian Panda flew atop Shiori. She could barely make out his round body atop the crane and smiled at the sight of it. Unlike the tigers, the Guardian Panda was not graced with an aerodynamic form.

Try as she might, she could not make out any of the scout birds, who blended perfectly into the onyx-dusted feathers of the cranes. She wondered how a squadron of such tiny birds could be helpful in Yuka's rescue.

Clara looked off into the distance. The sky was still dark. Sunrise would be approaching in a few hours, and darkness was their only element of surprise. From her vantage point, Clara could only see that the terrain that they were flying over was dark and barren. When the moonbeams cut through for a fleeting moment, Clara caught the sheen reflected off the glass-like terrain of The Shards. It looked forbidding, but she wondered what the terrain was like up close. She imagined jagged crystals bursting through the glassy ground, ready to shatter at any moment.

Clara's ears perked up as several soft calls were exchanged among the cranes. Clara looked up as the Guardian Crane whispered, "There it is."

Clara peered over the Guardian Crane's shoulder and in the distance, she saw the faint outline of a large structure jutting out from the side of a mountain. Faint glowing light emanated from several locations along its walls. *The Warlock's fortress,* she thought. She looked down and saw a dark forest surrounding the terrain beneath the fortress. Lost in thought, she hadn't even noticed the sudden transition from The Shards into Nadi. She wondered what else may be hidden in the darkness below.

"Empress Warrior Wu," said the Guardian Crane.

"Yes?" responded Clara.

"While we are still far out, please power up the Bamboo Jade, and let's hope that it will work," asked the Guardian Crane.

Clara nodded. She thought about the moment when she first powered up the new Bamboo Jade on the Jade Floor as her thumb glided over the jade. And despite the jade being hidden beneath the onyx powder, a white bead of light swirled out and flashed in a fleeting moment before it was gone. She nervously hoped that the momentary flash of light did not ruin their element of surprise.

"Did it work?" asked Clara as she looked over to where she thought the Guardian Panda was.

"We won't know until the arrows are used," the Guardian Crane replied. "Let's hope so."

Clara looked about her to the other members of the rescue team and asked quietly, "But the other cranes and the tigers, their armor is not protected?"

A moment passed through the air as the Guardian Crane spoke, "Yes, once we passed over The Shards, the Prowlers blue jade became inert while our jade's power went inert some time back. We will only have our battle armor and weapons to protect us."

Clara nodded quietly as her thumb rubbed the Bamboo Jade as she snuck a furtive glance at her Guardian Panda.

The cranes extended their wings, slowing themselves down as they quietly glided toward the fortress. There was an unsettling eeriness all about them as the Warlock's fortress loomed closer. The cranes were still several hundred feet up when they assumed a silent circular flight formation.

Clara pushed away from the Guardian Crane just a bit to look at the circular formation of the five cranes as the sleek bodies of the tigers lifted from their backs. With a flick of their wrists, onyx-dusted Clawdium blades extended from the tigers' paws and locked into place with a sharp click. The Guardian Panda unslung his bow and placed it snugly at his belly. Clara peered down at her bow and sensed the comfort of the Bamboo Jade. She gripped it and unslung it as she rested it in front of her.

Clara suddenly tuned in to a mass of fluttering wings as several tiny blacked-out birds converged in the center of the circular flight formation. Without a sound, the squadron of tiny scout birds spiraled silently downward toward the forbidding fortress.

Michi raced downward ahead of her squadron. When the squadron descended fifty feet, one of the birds in the rear stayed behind. After the next fifty feet, another bird stayed hovering in place.

Michi scanned the Warlock's fortress for the first time. Finally, here was the infamous fortress that she had only heard of in stories. The roof of the fortress's longer wing seemed to be covered in slate shingles, while the shorter wing was covered in glass.

Her keen eyes spotted several chimneys along the slate-shingled roof. Most of the windows carved into the stone were open, and a soft glow emanated from them. No one from Azen had ever gotten this close to the Warlock's fortress, so the Warlock had no need to worry about intruders. But the complacency cultivated over centuries meant opportunity for Michi and her squadron. Michi noticed that there were no guards visible.

Michi pulled in and then re-extended her left wing as five birds broke off and flew toward the chimneys. Those birds then separated and silently dove into the five chimney flues. Michi flew toward the center of the fortress as the remaining squadron broke off into four groups of ten birds. Each group then silently flew through an open window.

Upon entering a large open hallway, Michi's group of ten birds quickly flew toward the ceiling and perched atop a wooden rafter. Michi scanned the outer hallway, which was paved in stone slabs, and the inner wall, which was lit with torches at regular intervals. There were arched doorways blocked by thick wooden doors with iron bracings. The rafter was just above an arched entrance that connected to the other part of the fortress. Michi was about to take off to search for Yuka when a hulking, snarling creature appeared from the doorway beneath them. Michi and the other blacked-out birds went silent as they pressed their bodies against the rafter.

Michi's tiny eyes widened as she saw a large tree passing beneath them, its roots silently dribbling along the stone floor as its twisted branches writhed in the air. It continued down the hall before entering one of the rooms. Michi flew off the rafter, leaving one bird behind while another flew toward the rooms down the hall to investigate. Michi flew into the main stairwell of the fortress, where a large set of stone stairs connected all the floors. There were doors on the left, and Michi was about to fly down the stairs when she spotted the backs of two demon dogs climbing up them.

Michi glanced into the adjacent structure, which was presumably the throne room. It was entirely open from the top floor to the ground level. In a heartbeat, Michi and seven blacked-out birds dove about one hundred feet into the deserted throne room. Seeing no one, Michi flew through the twenty-foot doorway followed by six scout birds, leaving one behind, where she discovered another cavernous structure carved into the mountainside. This had not been visible from the outside.

Michi caught sight of several demon trees and fire demon dogs roaming about, and along with her squadron, flew toward the ceiling to avoid detection. Michi then flew into the inset structure with large doorways on the left and right, racing ahead unnoticed. The other six birds broke off and started to quickly survey all the other rooms.

Michi had a hunch and flew straight ahead to the last room on the left. As she hovered in front of the doorway, her eyes bulged. Yuka was lying face down on a stone slab table with a creature she assumed to be the Warlock looming over her as two demon trees stood close by.

Michi flew from the door and quickly encountered a member from her squadron and exchanged a message in a few hushed chirps. That scout bird then raced away until it came upon the scout bird who had stayed behind at the doorway to the throne room, who then flew to find the next scout bird. Michi flew back to the room that Yuka was in and observed quietly. *"Hurry!"* she thought.

The Harvester stared at the ghastly reddish-purplish skin that had been sucked up by the glass cups. He plucked off the last glass with a loud pop. Yuka's once-unblemished back was covered with ten round purple welts. Yuka's writhed feebly as the Harvester quickly slipped a flat metal square under the glass and presented it to the Warlock, who greedily inhaled its contents. He grunted with displeasure as he threw the glass onto the stone floor, shattering it to pieces along with the others.

"Nothing!" bemoaned the Warlock as he looked angrily at the cowering Harvester. He turned his angry glare at Yuka's near-lifeless and defeated body. "It's got to be inside of her. Gut her."

The Harvester looked up with its frowning glowing eyes and protested, "But my Lord, that will certainly kill her."

The Warlock turned to him, "I don't care! We've tried your way, now we'll try mine. Before she dies, gut her!"

"But my Lord, we could learn so much more if we keep her alive and…"

"Silence! Gut her," said the Warlock as he beamed at the Harvester and placed his hand on the handle of a sheathed blade at his waist. As he pulled the glistening white blade a quarter of the way out, but the Harvester tree waved one of its branches.

"We won't need the Oblivion Blade, my Lord," said the Harvester reverently.

The Warlock looked deeply into the Harvester's nervous glowing yellowish eyes as the Harvester said, "The Oblivion Blade's purpose would be ill-suited for this task. Besides, we have already removed the white jade from her outfit and depriving it of its protective abilities."

The Warlock sighed and re-sheathed the white Oblivion Blade as he said ominously, "Give me her heart."

The Harvester nodded reluctantly as the captor tree roughly flipped Yuka's limp body over. Its branches slithered over her. As the Harvester tree skittered away on its roots, it reluctantly said. "Yes, my Lord."

Upon reaching the back table, the Harvester opened a wooden box and removed the item within—a menacing, curved shiny blade. Just as the tree was about to return to Yuka, several chirps sounded from the doorway, causing the tree to look up as several black birds flew in aggressively, distracting the Harvester from his work.

"What is this!?" growled the Warlock as he swiped through the air at the fluttery nuisances.

The anxious scout bird on the topmost rafter got the message and urgently flew out of the window into the darkest of night. It chirped frantically at the next scout bird. That scout bird then flew up as fast it could to the next bird, relaying the message until the last scout bird flew into the middle of the circular crane formation.

Clara couldn't understand the frenzied chirps, but just knew the message was urgent. The Guardian Crane listened intently and suddenly broke the circular formation as she folded her wings inward. The jolt caused Clara's heart to jump as the Guardian Crane shouted *dive* in Japanese to the Top Talon members: "*Tsukkome!*"

As the Guardian Crane dove, she picked up incredible speed toward the glass roof as she yelled to Clara, "Brace yourself!"

Clara pressed herself into the Guardian Crane's body as she brought her wings forward, bringing the tips of the *katana* wings together. The Guardian Crane crashed through the glass roof as shards of glass rained down toward the stone floor. Once through, the four other cranes swooshed in. In a mere instant, a scout bird caught the eye of the Guardian Crane and chirped loudly. As the first shard of glass fell toward the stone floor below, it was swept up in the gust of air created as the Guardian Crane's swooped quickly into the throne room. Her sleek body ripped through the air and into the structure set into the mountain. Frantic chirps could be heard all around as the Guardian Crane sped toward the last room on the left.

A pair of demon dogs raced out of one of the rooms on the left and down the hallway toward the Guardian Crane, snapping their jaws. She unfurled her *katana* wings and sliced through them as the top and bottom halves of their bodies collapsed in a bloody mess of entrails.

The Guardian Crane banked left, and her beady eyes lit up at the sight of Yuka on the stone slab, held in place by the branches of a howling demon tree. She caught sight of the Harvester, who was frantically waving a shiny curved blade into the air as it tried to swat at the flurry of scout birds. But her eyes finally glanced at the Warlock for the first time as she flew desperately toward Yuka.

Clara gasped at the sight of Yuka and was about to reach for an arrow when the Warlock struck the Guardian Crane's chest, sending her backwards. In a split second, Clara unfastened her harness and pushed off the Guardian Crane's back, flipping backwards and landing on the ground in a crouch. Her gaze met that of the Warlock, who realized suddenly that another warrior was in his presence.

He rumbled toward Clara as Shiori flew over her, just barely grazing the top of her helmet as the Guardian Panda leapt off and barreled into the Warlock with his full weight. But this sent the Warlock back only a couple of steps as the black mass that was the Guardian Panda bounced off him and landed in front of Clara.

The Guardian Panda saw the Guardian Crane readying for another flyby when he yelled to Clara, "The tree's eyes!"

Clara nodded, pulled out two blacked-out jade-tipped arrows, and sent them toward the captor tree. Each arrow sunk into its glowing eyes, causing the tree to howl in agony as it retracted all of it branches.

The Ox Head, along with two fire demon dogs, entered through a door in the far corner and saw the mayhem. It looked up at the Warlock, who barked, "Kill the wretched creatures, but capture the warrior alive!"

The Warlock glared at the Harvester tree and ordered, "Gut her now! I will deal with these intruders myself!"

The Warlock unsheathed a massive double-edged sword from his back and raised it upwards as the Harvester skittered across the floor toward Yuka with the sinister curved blade. An arrow suddenly hit the blade, flicking it out of its branch. Looking to see where the arrow had come from, the Harvester spotted Clara loading another arrow.

The Guardian Panda sent arrow after arrow toward the Warlock, who deflected them with his armored gauntlet. He was growing increasingly annoyed by the arrows as the Guardian Crane swished by.

The Guardian Crane focused on Yuka, extending her talons. In an instant, she gripped Yuka by the armpits, whisked her off the stone table, and circled left. The two *Huo Dou* demon dogs, fire forming at their mouths, leapt upward just as a dark shape flew between them with its wings extended. Their halved bodies slumped lifelessly to the ground as the Ox Head threw himself onto his back to avoid the same fate. Shiori then circled back.

The Guardian Crane shrieked as she flew toward the door just as the Warlock swung his sword at her. She extended her left *katana* wing to meet the Warlock's sword as explosive sparks flew everywhere. The Guardian Crane's wing buckled momentarily, but not before she flew by the Warlock and out the door. She flew over three blacked-out Prowler tigers as they slashed and stabbed at the fire demon dogs, denying them entry into the examination room.

Shiori quickly landed near Clara and screamed, "Get on!" Clara frantically secured herself and grasped onto the harness, eyeing the Guardian Panda, who had stepped between her and the Warlock with worry as he fired his last arrow at him.

"Guardian Panda!" screamed Clara as Shiori violently lifted off as another crane flew underneath them. It executed a hard turn and made a hard landing by the Guardian Panda, who jumped onto its back just as the Warlock and the Ox Head ran after them. The crane flapped hard and lurched through the door, away from the clutches of the Warlock and the Ox Head.

The largest of the cranes had just sliced off the top branches of a demon tree that it was battling in the large hallway and caught sight of three cranes swooshing by, as the Warlock appeared just beyond the doorway. It shrieked toward the two closest tigers, who retracted their blades and jumped onto its back, the first tiger gripping the harness while the second held onto the first with all his might. Despite struggling with the tigers' combined weight, the crane managed to take off as the fifth crane swooped in toward the last tiger and screamed, "Jump!" The tiger retracted his blades, leapt forward, and landed on the crane's back just as two fire demon dogs caught up to them. The crane extended her *katana* wings and sliced through them as it soared upward after the rest of the cranes.

The scout birds were rallying in chaotic chirps as they raced after the cranes. The fortress was in utter chaos as fire demon dogs and trees scattered.

The Guardian Crane, with Yuka dangling precariously in her talons, entered the throne room and swooped upward through the shattered opening of the glass roof as loose shards of glass flew upwards in her wake.

Clara was next. She pressed her legs against Shiori's body as she lurched upward when suddenly, gnarly branches formed a web in front of them, blocking their path. Shiori shrieked and banked violently toward the throne. Clara glanced downward and her eyes caught the Moon Star *shuriken* standing upright on the throne's left armrest.

"The Moon Star is on the armrest!" Clara screamed as she pointed in the throne's direction. "We have to get it!"

Shiori nodded and flew toward the throne. Clara hooked her left arm under the harness and extended her right hand as the crane folded in her right wing. Shiori began to spiral left as Clara's eyes locked onto the Moon Star, and in an instant, she was upside down. Reaching down, she snatched up the Moon Star just as her eyes passed over the dark glassy orb on the other armrest. Shiori came out of the spiral, and as Clara looked to her right, she gasped. Mounted on the wall were the skeletal remains of several cranes. Shiori continued banking left and upward toward the opening in the glass roof. Looking backwards, Clara glanced at the five stone pedestals.

The demon tree that had blocked the shattered glass opening before was howling. Its branches had been shorn off and lay on the floor where they'd fallen after the Guardian Panda's crane had sliced through them. Shiori whisked through the opening in the ceiling. The crane with the two tigers struggled but made it past the shattered glass. It was soon followed by the crane with the last tiger, and lastly, the crane with the Guardian Panda. Soon, amidst a flutter of tiny wings, the scouts flew through as well, leaving the frustrated Warlock looking up from the floor of the throne room.

"Empress Warrior Wu," said Shiori as Clara's heart pounded within her chest.

"Yes?! Yes?" Clara asked as her mind was still trying to absorb the harrowing escape that she'd just experienced. Everything happened so fast.

"Secure the Moon Star *shuriken* and check that you are harnessed in," Shiori said.

Clara snapped out of her daze and still panting, she carefully tucked the Moon Star behind her chest plate. She found that her hands were trembling as the cool night air whisked by her face.

"Good," said Shiori. "Now, on my backside of my battle suit, you should find a flap. Pull it open and pull out the robe."

Clara was puzzled but she reached back and found the flap. She opened it and pulled out a folded black robe.

"What's the robe for?" asked Clara.

"For Empress Warrior Satoh," said the crane gravely. "We need to retrieve her body in midair from the Guardian Crane."

Clara looked upward, startled, and realized Shiori was flying directly under the Guardian Crane. Then she saw Yuka dangling from her talons.

"Yuka!" Clara cried out as she quickly tucked the cloak in between her waist and the harness.

"The Guardian Crane is going to lower her to you," said Shiori. "You'll need to pull her in, secure her with the secondary harness, and drape the robe over her body."

Clara choked back the tears that suddenly clogged her throat as she answered, "Yes. I got her."

The Guardian Crane heard a few squawks and flew steadily as Shiori flew underneath her. Clara looked up at Yuka as her body dangled above her. Her tattered, fluttering clothing made her look so fragile. *"What did they do to you?"* Clara thought to herself. As Yuka's feet came within reach, Clara pulled on Yuka's cold ankles and gently eased her down.

"Yuka!" screamed Clara, but Yuka did not respond. Her eyes were closed, and her hair was splayed across her face. Yuka's cold body was finally firmly pressed up against hers. "I got her!"

The Guardian Crane released her grip just as the Guardian Panda flew up to Clara's right. His eyes looked at Clara with heartache.

"Yuka," Clara pleaded through her sobs as Yuka's arms dangled lifelessly at her sides. Clara supported Yuka's neck as she looked at her. "Wake up. Please!"

"Empress Warrior Wu," said the Guardian Crane.

Clara pulled Yuka into her body allowing her head to rest on her shoulder. She looked over at the Guardian Crane.

"Is Empress Warrior Satoh alive?" she asked gravely.

Clara pulled Yuka in and pressed her chest against hers. She nestled her ear close to Yuka's nostrils as she gently held the back of her head. She didn't hear anything at first, but soon heard Yuka's shallow breathing. Clara felt her heart jump in relief.

"She's alive!" hollered Clara to the Guardian Crane, who nodded.

"We weren't too late," said the Guardian Crane. "Please harness her in and drape her in the robe."

Clara nodded, carefully pulled out the secondary harness, and secured Yuka. She unfurled the robe and fumbled with it in the wind. As she looked at Yuka's back, she saw the reddish-purplish welts and gasped. "*What did they do to you!*" she screamed in her mind. But she put aside her concerns as she wrapped the robe around Yuka.

"Empress Warrior Wu," said the Guardian Panda.

"Yes?" asked Clara.

"Use your Qi," said the Guardian Panda. "Replenish her Qi."

Clara nodded and inhaled. She slipped her hands underneath the robe and placed them right between Yuka's shoulder blades.

"Don't worry, Yuka," said Clara softly. "I got you."

Clara closed her eyes and reached inward to feel her own Qi. She easily found it, as she had become more in tune with it. She could feel its warming sensation through her body, and she channeled that warmth through her arms and finally her hands. Clara's Qi then flowed freely from her hands into Yuka's cold body. The Qi traveled deep into Yuka's body and soon, Yuka's Qi started to pulse.

Yuka gasped softly, and Clara smiled as she felt a slight jolt in Yuka's chest. She opened her teary eyes and nodded at the Guardian Crane.

Clara continued to gently caress Yuka's back when she heard a murmur.

She placed her ear close to Yuka's face and asked gently, "Yes Yuka?"

"Help me…" was all Yuka could manage under her breath.

Clara teared up and pulled Yuka closer, "You're safe now. I got you."

The five cranes continued their arduous journey back just as the sunrise started to crest over the eastern horizon.

NINETEEN

Clara held Yuka's limp and barely warm body tightly, trying to share her own warmth. She gently caressed Yuka's back, trying to give her reassurance. Aside from a few unintelligible murmurings, she was asleep.

"Hold on," Clara whispered as she quieted her churning emotions and wiped her teary eyes. Though she tried to stay calm as she held Yuka, the anger within her welled up and she wanted to think it generated body warmth to help Yuka. *How awful the Warlock was to have tortured Yuka, who's so sweet and innocent!* How she wished she had more time to send her arrows into the Warlock and the howling demon trees who were doing unspeakable things to her. The rescue itself had been a blur, but Clara clearly remembered hearing the Warlock order, "Gut her now!"

They were mere moments from losing Yuka, and her mind drifted to the tragic horror had they not reached her in time. Her thoughts also turned to Daniel and her anger at him flared again. *It was all his fault*, she thought. *Why couldn't he listen and respect the rules laid out by the Guardians of Azen?*

Yuka murmured. Clara cleared away her tangled thoughts as she looked at her, who was still asleep. Clara exhaled and gently repositioned Yuka's head on her shoulder while she repositioned her grip on the harness. As she did, she saw the deep impression of the harness in her right open palm. She must not have noticed her clenched fist as the angry thoughts coursed through her mind.

She looked up and shifted to her right. The Guardian Crane was in the lead, while the Guardian Panda and his crane were behind to her left. To her right were the other two cranes. The one in the second position was ferrying two tigers, and the last crane had just the one. Michi, along with her scout birds, were evenly divided among the cranes, resting in small groups along the cranes' necks. They were flying at a much lower altitude; their energy was spent from the breakneck speed at reaching the Warlock's fortress, the ferocious battle that they had engaged in, and now the exhausting flight home.

The crane with the two tigers was beginning to show signs of exhaustion. Still, Clara knew they wanted to avoid the risk of landing on The Shards, knowing that their sole objective was to hurry back to the northern battlefront as soon as possible. With the sun rising behind them, they were only a few hours away from noon—the time when the kingdom armies would all need to gather at the northern battlefront to fight the third Warlock army.

Clara heard startled grunts and a shriek to her right, where she saw the two tigers rebalancing themselves atop the exhausted crane. The crane steadied himself in flight and let out a few calls, to which the Guardian Crane responded to. The Guardian Crane was silent for a moment before letting out a few more calls and pointing her beak downward toward The Shards.

"Empress Warrior Wu," said Shiori.

"Yes?" asked Clara.

"We're going to land for a moment. Please hold onto Empress Warrior Satoh."

Clara nodded and tugged on the harnesses, ensuring that they were secure. The cranes opened their wings and began their slow descent. Clara turned to her Guardian Panda and with the early sunlight, she could see him in his entire blacked-out gear. His brown eyes behind the black furry eye patches blinked a few times as his crane also began his descent.

Clara looked down at the glassy terrain of The Shards. The flow of the obsidian terrain stretched north to south, and violent gashes formed deep, dark crevasses. Some shards shot up like jagged knives. It was unlike anything she had ever seen, but it was eerily beautiful as well.

The Guardian Crane aimed for a clearing in The Shards as the rest followed in formation. Her beady eyes focused, and soon she opened her wings. Her talons touched lightly on The Shards. The other cranes also landed softly. There was a collective sigh of relief as everyone scanned the surrounding terrain. Nothing but a glassy, lifeless obsidian wasteland. There was no sound at all.

As the Guardian Crane stepped toward Clara, one of the two tigers leapt off the tired crane to take his weight off him. But as he landed, his soft paws started to slide on the glassy surface, and he instinctively extended his claws to steady himself. An ominous cracking sound caught everyone's attention, and the tiger looked up in shock as the glassy terrain beneath him splintered away and slid into the crevasse, pulling him downward. The air was filled with a deafening roar as large pieces of the glassy terrain cracked apart, but the tiger's howling roar of fear was even more agonizing. The Guardian Crane shrieked and gave a desperate order to ascend.

Clara was jolted upward, and she pulled Yuka in tightly as Shiori's massive wings flapped upward. Clara looked hopelessly to where the tiger had disappeared into the crevasse and suddenly saw the Guardian Crane diving into it. Silence descended on the area once more as everyone's eyes fixed on the tiger's last location. Soon, the massive wings of the Guardian Crane flapped upwards. As she slowly ascended, the nape of the tiger appeared in her talons. The tiger wore a catatonic gaze, his front paws pulled in while his rear legs and tail were curled upwards.

The crane that had flown the two tigers swiftly flew underneath the Guardian Crane, who carefully lowered the tiger into the waiting paws of his fellow tiger. As soon as she released her talons from his nape, the tiger suddenly came to and shook his furry head before gripping the harness.

The Guardian Crane flew upward and scanned the terrain once more. She called a few times and flew to another clearing in The Shards with everyone following. The Guardian Crane slowly descended and landed softly, onto its webbed feet with her talons slightly lifted. She called out instructions to the rest of the cranes.

"Empress Warrior Wu," said Shiori. "We need to land carefully. Guardian Crane believes the tiger's claws unintentionally cracked The Shards."

"Got it," said Clara as she nodded.

Soon, all four cranes managed to land without cracking the hard yet delicate shards. The tigers remained on their cranes as everyone stayed alert, paranoid that the glassy shards beneath them could break away at any time.

The Guardian Crane, along with the crane carrying the Guardian Panda, walked carefully over to Clara.

"How is she, Empress Warrior Wu?" asked the worried Guardian Crane.

Clara looked at the Guardian Crane as she softly rubbed Yuka's back. "I don't know, to be honest. She's alive, but she's so weak. She seems to be asleep most of the time."

"How much further?" asked the Guardian Panda.

"I took my last star bearing before sunrise," said the Guardian Crane before pausing. "Since we're flying much lower and slower, I think we are only one third of the way to Azen."

"That's all?" asked the Guardian Panda with dismay.

"I'm afraid so," said the Guardian Crane.

"What does that mean?" asked Clara.

The Guardian Crane looked up at Clara and replied, "At this speed, we will be late to the battle."

"Oh no!" said Clara as a sense of hopelessness filled her.

"My cranes are fatigued, and there is no water. The Prowlers are no better, as the battle has worn them down," said the Guardian Crane.

The Guardian Panda shook his head, "At least we all made it out with Empress Warrior Satoh, but I fear time is not on our side."

"No, it is not," said the Guardian Crane. "We'll rest for 15 minutes, and we'll push on. I can take the Empress Warriors, and the other tiger can fly on Shiori."

"Can we do anything for Empress Warrior Satoh?" asked the Guardian Panda.

The Guardian Crane looked at the unresponsive Yuka and lowered her head, "I don't know. We have to get her back to Crane Castle and let the herbalist look her over."

Over an eerie silence, the Guardian Panda helped move Clara and Yuka onto the back of the Guardian Crane. Shiori flew to the tiger who had fallen into the crevasse and allowed him to climb onto her back. Soon, the cranes lifted off once more toward Azen. The Guardian Crane was in the lead once more, leading the exhausted rescue team.

Clara stared anxiously ahead, hoping that she could see the end of The Shards and Azen beyond it. It would have been a welcome sight, she thought. Yuka murmured and Clara pulled her in tighter. Clara was suddenly distracted by black dust that was fluttering into her face. She closed her eyes to shield them, but through her squints, she could see that the black dust was flying up from the Guardian Crane. The onyx powder was shedding. She looked at the upper arc of her bow and it too began to shed the onyx powder, revealing the beautiful bamboo sheen of the Bow of Destiny. Clara looked about curiously as she saw the black onyx powder flying off the cranes, the tigers, and finally her Guardian Panda. She couldn't help but giggle once more as the blacked-out body suit he was wearing was not flattering, but at least, his white fur was again visible. Her eyes caught sight of the majestic red feathers atop the Guardian Crane's head. It was a beacon of hope, forging its way over The Shards, back to Azen.

But only an hour passed before the tired rescue squad was forced to land atop the precarious shards once more. After some cautious attempts, the cranes were able to rest on their bellies as their heads drooped. All the tigers could do were to stay atop their winged warriors. The cranes' throats were parched.

Though the Guardian Crane tried to not show it, she showed signs of fatigue as well. But her mind was preoccupied with the well-being of her Crane Warrior. They reluctantly decided to rest for an hour, and the Guardian Crane estimated they were only halfway through The Shards. But every minute longer on The Shards was more time taken away from the care that Yuka needed.

"Don't worry, Yuka," said Clara soothingly as she gently rocked Yuka atop the Guardian Crane. "We'll get you back to Crane Castle, and you'll be fine."

The Guardian Crane looked back as one of her beady eyes met Clara's. "How is Empress Warrior Satoh?"

"I don't know," Clara said. "It's not like when I replenished Sung's Qi. This time, it's different. She seems to be getting weaker. What should I do?"

"Her Qi," the Guardian Panda said guardedly. "It must be imbalanced."

Clara looked perplexed and glanced at the Guardian Crane.

"What do you suggest?" asked the Guardian Crane.

"The Healing Pool," said the Guardian Panda.

Clara looked at the Guardian Panda with curiosity and asked, "Another mystical water pool?"

The Guardian Crane nodded and began, "Yes. It's another mystical pool, but this one is different. In this pool is a tranquil island, and on it, is a large tree whose leaves are made of gold. It never sheds its leaves except when a cure is needed. Its highly medicinal properties have helped a few select warriors, guardians, and kingdom leaders in the past."

"Can this tree help Yuka?" asked Clara.

"It might," continued the Guardian Crane. "But there is no guarantee. But it's also out of our way, and the wait could be long."

"We have to try," the Guardian Panda urged. "For Empress Warrior Satoh."

"I don't know if the rest of the squadron can make the long flight," said the Guardian Crane despondently.

"You don't need them to go with you," said the Guardian Panda as the Guardian Crane looked in his direction. "The rescue is over. The remaining cranes and tigers can take their time to return to Azen. We can fly to the Healing Pool."

The Guardian Crane was deep in thought. She looked at Clara holding Yuka, then back at the Guardian Panda when a shriek from above caught her attention.

Everyone looked up and to their delight, saw five eagles descending towards them.

The Guardian Crane exhaled with relief, looked back up, and called a few times to the descending eagles. The eagles called back in understanding. The lead eagle descended slowly and gently landed on the tips of its feet without cracking the shards.

As the lead eagle approached, a familiar white-and-black striped creature rose from its back. It was the Guardian Tiger, who wore an expression of worry and relief. He eked out a grin and looked at the Guardian Crane. "I bet you are glad to see me," he said genially.

The Guardian Crane smiled and responded graciously, "Yes I am, Yonggirang."

The Guardian Tiger looked at the Guardian Panda and uttered, "Old friend."

"Old friend indeed," said the Guardian Panda.

The Guardian Tiger looked at Clara and Yuka and asked of the Guardian Crane, "Empress Warrior Satoh?"

"Alive," said the Guardian Crane grimacing.

The Guardian Tiger reached behind him for a bamboo water container. With a motion of the Guardian Crane's beak, the Guardian Tiger's eagle moved toward Clara, who eagerly took the bamboo water container. Clara gently lay Yuka down on the back of the Guardian Crane. She carefully brought the rim of the bamboo container to Yuka's lips and let a few drops dribble onto them. Yuka's lips did not move. Clara then carefully parted her lips and allowed a short stream to flow into her dry mouth. Yuka instinctively swallowed it. Clara did it again, but Yuka coughed. Clara pulled back in worry. But the cough passed as Yuka's eyes finally opened. She blinked a few times against the sunlight and through her squints, mumbled, "Clara?"

"Don't talk, Yuka," Clara said soothingly. "Here, just drink."

Clara gently lifted Yuka as the Guardian Panda approached and lent a supportive paw. Clara nodded appreciatively as she gently eased more water into Yuka's mouth. Her thirst was insatiable. For the first time since the rescue, Clara smiled.

Yuka shook her head, and though she was still weak, she turned her head and looked at the Guardian Crane with her tired eyes.

"Guardian Crane?" Yuka said weakly to which the Guardian Crane responded, "I'm here, Empress Warrior Satoh. We have you."

Yuka nodded as she rested her head on Clara's shoulder once more. "Where are we?"

"We rescued you from the Warlock," said Clara. "We're headed back to another pool to heal you."

Yuka abruptly broke down as newfound tears seeped along her closed eyelids. "The Warlock, he hurt me," said Yuka through a sob.

Clara instinctively pulled Yuka tighter. She was heartbroken over the pain that Yuka must be reliving in her mind and feeling throughout her battered body. She couldn't even imagine her torture. She recalled that the closest to mortal danger that she had ever experienced was when she was alone in the forest before the first battle. If Yuka hadn't saved her life that night, she might not have been there for Yuka.

"You saved me," Clara whispered into Yuka's ear. "Now we're going to save you."

Clara looked up at the guardians in front of her and declared, "Let's go to the Healing Pool."

TWENTY

Clara was eager to leave the barren and brittle Shards. Before they lifted off to race toward the Healing Pool, she pressed her hand onto the glassy obsidian surface and could not perceive even a speck of dirt. Her earth Wu Qi elemental powers were rendered powerless in such a lifeless place. As her fingertips glided along the glassy terrain, she could sense its brittleness and wondered about its mysterious ability to grow back. *How?* she thought.

With the help of the Guardian Panda, who was certain his padded feet would not break the shards, they replaced Yuka's clothing. As Clara changed her out of her violently torn clothing, Clara was aghast at the sight of the purplish and reddish round welts along her back. A mixture of horror, grief, and anger welled up from deep within. Though she was familiar with the welts from traditional Chinese medicinal cupping techniques, these were different. These were evil. She hurriedly changed Yuka into a comfortable tunic, pants, socks, and shoes.

Once aboard the Guardian Crane, Yuka had fallen into a deep sleep, but at least she now had the strength to drape her arms over Clara's shoulders. Clara held onto her waist with one hand and the harness in the other. After they refastened all the harnesses, Clara readjusted Yuka's robe as she put on a green robe herself, and they were ready to fly off.

The Guardian Tiger explained that as much faith he had in the Guardian Crane and her Top Talon cranes, he kept pacing with worry back in Azen. To alleviate his worry, he consulted with the head of the Top Talon team, Sho, and was given the approval to mount a rendezvous mission with the five eagles to bring much-needed supplies, especially water and food. The Guardian Crane and Panda were also grateful for his forethought. Though the Guardian Crane had been hesitant to admit it, she had feared that not all of them may have had the energy to safely return to Crane Castle. But once the other cranes, scout birds, and tigers had replenished themselves with fresh water and food, the tigers mounted the eagles along with the Guardian Tiger to fly back to the battlefront.

Despite admonishment from the Guardian Crane, the four cranes insisted on continuing to escort Empress Warrior Satoh. In the face of such loyalty, the Guardian Crane relented. The Guardian Crane also knew it'd be futile to argue with the Guardian Panda, as he had a duty to protect Clara. Michi and her scout birds clambered onto the back of the last two cranes. Once all the details were settled, they took off from The Shards one last time.

After some flying, they were relieved to be back in Azen. The cranes and the eagles called back and forth to each other, the eagles flying north while the cranes turned south. Clara looked up and saw that the sun was almost overhead—noon was near. The land battle forces would have just arrived at the northern battlefront to mount the defenses. As it was a sea battle, the naval forces of the Buffalo Kingdom were already deployed to form a blockade against the forces of the Warlock. But that would only be temporary.

Yuka murmured in her sleep, and Clara gently pulled her in, sharing her body warmth when she felt a slight jab against her stomach. She let out a slight gasp, let go of the harness, and gently reached into her chest plate. She carefully pulled out the Moon Star. Her eyes rested on the dull white jade. An expression of worry came upon her face.

"Guardian Crane," beckoned Clara.

The Guardian Crane's eyes rolled back momentarily, and she replied, "Yes, Empress Warrior Wu?"

"The white jade," said Clara. "It isn't glowing."

There was a pause and the Guardian Crane replied, "Yes, I suspected as much when I noticed our own jades didn't glow as we crossed back into Azen despite having Empress Warrior Satoh with us. She will need to activate it but in her weakened state, I do not know if she will be able to."

"You don't know?"

"I can't know what I do not understand," said the Guardian Crane sadly. "But I would guess that Empress Warrior Satoh's injuries are more than just corporeal."

"I don't understand," said Clara as she carefully tucked the Moon Star back into her chest plate.

"I don't have answers for you, Empress Warrior Wu," said the Guardian Crane before she continued with a more hopeful tone. "I can only hope that the Healing Pool will restore Empress Warrior Satoh to her rightful self."

"Her Qi," said Clara.

"Yes," replied the Guardian Crane.

Clara nodded as she pulled Yuka in closer as she whispered, "Rest, Yuka. You'll be fine," to which Yuka murmured quietly.

The Top Talon rescue squad flew silently and swiftly until Clara heard the ocean. She looked outward and saw that the southern tip of Azen ended in a high bluff above an ocean whose waves crashed below. As they flew beyond it, she could feel the shift from land air to ocean air and inhaled its saltiness. To her right, she could see that the southern tip of Azen curved into a steep and long mountainous peninsula, with pillars of rocks rising into the air. Somewhere in there must be the southern battlefront, she surmised.

Clara's attention was distracted by a few crane calls and she turned around to see that the two cranes at the end of the V formation had peeled off toward a large island.

"There's Red Crown Crane Kingdom," said the Guardian Crane to Clara.

Clara looked curiously as she saw a large, blackened island with an abundance of green scattered across its terrain. As she squinted, she could see pagoda-like structures peeking out. As they flew by the island, Clara could see the large remnants of a collapsed volcano. At the center was the famed Red Crown Crane Castle that Yuka constantly raved about.

"Is that Crane Castle?" asked Clara just as its large, tiered red roofs passed beneath the wings of the Guardian Crane.

"Yes, Empress Warrior Wu," said the Guardian Crane. "You have not visited our majestic castle yet, have you?"

"No, I have not," said Clara with dismay. "I've been meaning to."

"Once Empress Warrior Satoh is well enough, all of you should visit our kingdom," offered the Guardian Crane. "It would be our honor."

"I would be honored," said Clara as she noticed the Guardian Crane turning in a southeasterly direction. "Yuka has mentioned so many beautiful things about it."

"I'm glad Empress Warrior Satoh enjoys her home here on Azen," the Guardian Crane replied.

"Are we close to the Healing Pool?" asked Clara as she gently readjusted her hold on Yuka.

"We are, Empress Warrior Wu," said the Guardian Crane. "The Healing Pool lies on a remote island southeast of Crane Castle. We should be there shortly."

"Okay," said Clara as she continued to admire the vast ocean beneath her.

Clara continued to hold onto Yuka atop the Guardian Crane. The Guardian Panda flew atop Shiori, and she was glad that he had returned to his usual white-and-black self. To her left was the third riderless crane, who looked majestic as the wind whisked over its black-and-white feathers and red crown.

But the peaceful flight belied the battle that Clara knew that Sung, Daniel, the Guardian Buffalo and Tiger would soon be engaged in—without them. She just hoped that they could heal Yuka in time for them to meet up with her fellow warriors and defeat the Warlock army to the north.

"There it is, Empress Warrior Wu," said the Guardian Crane.

Clara looked ahead and she saw it: A smaller island with a small peak. It was entirely black except for one spot, which was bright with green with tinges of purple, red, and yellow. She also saw two tall, slender towers peeking out from the mesh of color.

"Are those pagodas?" asked Clara.

The Guardian Crane's beady eyes shifted backward before returning to the front. "Oh, in Japanese, those pagoda-like towers are called *gō*. Those are guard towers; we have two squadrons of cranes that protect the Healing Pool at all times."

"I see," replied Clara as she could feel the Guardian Crane descending toward the small island. "Hold on, Empress Warrior Wu."

The three cranes soon leveled out on approach to the island, and Clara focused straight ahead. Closer to the ocean, the sound of the large waves was deafening. The upper tiers of the two gō towers were soon alit with activity. Several cranes called, and in response, the Guardian Crane let out a series of short and long calls. *A password*, thought Clara, as she imagined that three fast cranes on approach was not what the sentry cranes were expecting.

The calls subsided, and soon the three cranes swiftly sailed down a passage lined with slender trees on each side with strange but beautiful purple, red, and yellow leaves. Their flight ruffled the leaves, as if they were applauding the arrival of the Guardian Crane and her escorts. Soon, the cranes dove down into a clearing where Clara could see a pool of water, much larger than the Origins Pool but equally serene. *The Healing Pool*, thought Clara as her eyes fell onto the singular voluminous tree in the middle. She gasped in amazement: The tree's branches were shimmering in golden leaves.

The cranes flew over the low stone wall that encircled the Healing Pool and deftly landed on the island as Clara simply looked up at the glistening golden leaves. Led by the Guardian Crane, the cranes briskly walked toward the tree until they were under its golden foliage.

"These leaves are made of gold?" asked a shocked Clara.

"Yes, Empress Warrior Wu," said the Guardian Crane. "They are indeed, and there is one other odd characteristic about this tree."

Clara looked down at the Guardian Crane who had craned her head slightly toward Clara and asked, "What is that?"

"It does not shed its leaves," said the Guardian Crane as she lowered herself onto her belly.

"Empress Warrior Wu," said the Guardian Panda who quickly dismounted from his crane and briskly arrived at the Guardian Crane's side. Clara, mesmerized by the shimmering golden leaves, looked down at the Guardian Panda's outstretched paws.

"Unharness Empress Warrior Satoh and gently ease her into my paws. We must hurry," the Guardian Panda said.

Clara nodded, and while still holding onto Yuka, unclipped her harness and gently eased her into the awaiting paws of the Guardian Panda. He gingerly carried her toward the trunk of the tree. Clara hopped off as the Guardian Crane rose and followed the Guardian Panda.

Clara followed the Guardian Panda with a sense of awe, wondering what other beautiful places there were on Azen. As she approached the tree, she saw that the trunk was colossal. Its bark was gnarled, with large knots high up on the trunk and thick lower branches stretching outward. It must be almost as old as time itself, she thought.

"What makes this tree so special?" asked Clara of the Guardian Crane.

"We're not quite sure, Empress Warrior Wu," replied the Guardian Crane. "It is known as the Longevity Tree. It is the only one of its kind, and we believe it existed before Azen. It may be one of the first living things on this world, as far as we know. But we do believe that because it is the only tree in the Healing Pool, it draws the pool's special qualities into itself."

"And that quality is its healing properties?" asked Clara.

"Yes, Empress Warrior Wu," said the Guardian Crane. "Some unexplained symbiotic relationship between the Longevity Tree and the Healing Pool helps those who are in need of healing powers that we cannot give."

The Guardian Panda stopped at the base of the tree and found a spot where he carefully leaned Yuka up against the trunk in a sitting position. She murmured as her eyes fluttered open slightly.

"Guardian Panda?" asked Yuka.

The Guardian Panda looked tenderly at Yuka. He responded soothingly, "Yes, it's me, Empress Warrior Satoh. Rest and conserve your strength."

Yuka slightly turned her attention to the Guardian Crane.

"Guardian Crane?" Yuka asked.

The Guardian Crane gave a worried smile and replied soothingly, "Yes Empress Warrior Satoh, it's me. We are going to get you all better soon."

Yuka then turned her head to see a familiar face and with a weak smile murmured, "Clara."

Clara knelt down and gently placed her hand on Yuka's shoulder, "Hey Yuka. You're safe now, but we're going to make you all better."

Yuka nodded as her head drooped. Worried, Clara reached for her bamboo water container, untwisted the cap, and gently eased water into Yuka's mouth. Yuka nodded and Clara pulled back the container. Yuka licked her lips and her eyes closed from exhaustion.

"What happens next?" asked Clara.

"Now. The tree decides," said the Guardian Crane.

"The tree decides?" asked a perplexed Clara.

"Yes, the tree will judge her," said the Guardian Crane. "We must leave Yuka here with the tree."

"But I don't understand," asked Clara.

"We don't understand it ourselves, but the Longevity Tree will judge the ailment," said the Guardian Crane as she backed away.

"Yes, Empress Warrior Wu," said the Guardian Panda. "We must leave the Healing Pool's perimeter so it's only it and Empress Warrior Satoh."

Still confused, Clara scanned her surroundings, taking in the glistening green vegetation sprouting up from the dirt, the golden sheen of light piercing through the leaves, and the blue water of the Healing Pool at the edge of the small island. Then she remembered the pools within Jade Labyrinth and she realized Yuka was going to be judged, not by ghostly crane monks, but by the tree. The tree was sentient, she realized.

"Wait!" exclaimed Clara as she knelt beside Yuka. She looked at Yuka's tired face and parted her splayed hair. She pressed her hands along Yuka's shoulder and traced them down her arms. Her hands felt along the robe's front edges to ensure that they were sealed to ward off the cold. Clara grasped Yuka's clammy hands and held them gently. Yuka opened her tired eyes and smiled faintly.

"Yuka," said Clara in a soothing voice as Yuka nodded once. "I don't know how this works, but starting right now, you need to think about your Japanese heritage. Think about food. Think about your family. If you hear questions inside your head, just answer them truthfully."

Clara looked down as she bit her lip before she looked back up into Yuka's tired face, "Remain true."

"Mmmm," was all Yuka said in a weak voice.

Clara nodded as a tear formed at the corner of her eye. She gently shook Yuka's hands and said, "We have to go. But we'll be right over there, so we won't be far."

Clara released her fingers from Yuka's cold hands and backed away before turning.

Yuka opened her eyes a sliver and watched as Clara climbed aboard the Guardian Crane. Soon, she and two cranes flew silently away. They landed a short distance away and turned toward her to keep vigil. Yuka eked out a smile and she looked up to see the wondrous golden leaves above her. A smile appeared on her face as she took in the sight and uttered the Japanese word for *beautiful,* "*utsukushī.*"

As Clara dismounted the Guardian Crane, her boots hit the ground with a light thud. The Guardian Panda also landed onto the ground as everyone turned their gaze toward Yuka, who was leaning silently up against the tree.

"What happens next?" asked Clara.

"A leaf," said the Guardian Crane.

Clara turned upward toward the Guardian Crane with a quizzical look. "A leaf?"

The Guardian Crane turned toward Clara and explained. "Yes, Empress Warrior Wu. As I explained before, the Longevity Tree does not shed its leaves, unlike the trees around us that do."

Clara quickly looked upon the ground and she saw a vibrant mixture of fallen purple, red, and yellow leaves.

As Clara looked back up, the Guardian Crane continued. "Once the Longevity Tree has judged what ails Empress Warrior Satoh, it will shed one leaf, and that will contain the medicine she needs. At least I hope it will."

"That's intense," said Clara as she looked back at Yuka. "So what do we do now?"

The Guardian Crane exhaled and said, "We wait."

TWENTY - ONE

The wooden planks along the deck of the battle vessel creaked in rhythm as the waves sloshed against its wooden hull. An eerie silence dominated the blockade of massive battle vessels, spread out among the tattered green limestone towers to provide a buffer between the northern waters and the beach.

Daniel, in his full battle armor, stood tall and silent with the Club Horn of *Kting Voar* across his back. He had been deployed to the northern battlefront as the Buffalo Kingdom's navy was finalizing its blockade. Hundreds of battle buffalos were also set up along the beach in full battle armor, ready to ram and gore any of the Warlock's demon creatures that made it to the beach.

The regiments of battle tigers with their extensible blades had arrived an hour ago and were forming their own line of defense behind the ramming buffalos. Somewhere among them was Sung. Daniel reminded himself sadly that these were the only two kingdom armies currently protected by their jades.

The battle pandas with their skilled archers and spearmen had not yet arrived, but he knew their arrival was imminent. Daniel looked overhead to see the squadrons of cranes and eagles. They were taking up positions atop the tall limestone pillars, even the moving ones. His thoughts went to Yuka as it had been over nine hours since the rescue team had embarked on their mission to save her. He fretted about how his own arrogance had endangered the armies of Azen, but more importantly, his friends. For a moment, he clenched the wooden rail before relaxing and exhaling.

He glanced to his right and saw the stern buffalo eyes of the vessel's captain staring outward, surveying the seemingly peaceful waters. Wrinkles etched his leathery skin under his eye and cheek area, showing how much sun he had endured as a seafarer. Beyond him was the Guardian Buffalo, who looked attentive and silent as he kept a careful watch on the waters around him. Both were anticipating something from the water.

Daniel looked down on the deck of the ship, which was outfitted with several harpoons. Several buffalos were also silently watching the ocean in front of them. His eyes traveled upward to the masts, and at the top of each was a large, menacing arched blade spanning port to starboard, which glinted in the sunlight. Crossing each arched blade at regular intervals were smaller razor-sharp blades.

Though Daniel could not see it, earlier he had heard mechanical gears within the bowels of the battle vessel. He was told that along the underside of each battle vessel, a metal chain-linked net was uncoiled into the watery depths creating a barrier.

Something skimmed the water to Daniel's left: A schooner passed; at its bow was a hunter and a harpoon crossbow. Its purpose was to hunt down any demon creatures that got through the blockade.

Loud cheers suddenly erupted from the beach as a flurry of bamboo-clad white-and-black creatures appeared at the top of the seawall along the bluff. The battle pandas had finally arrived, and Daniel sighed in relief. Large, stocky green bamboo towers—something he had not seen before—slowly came into view as they were wheeled up along the seawall. As each one butted up against the stone seawall, a heavy Clawdium spike at the base of each tower slowly sunk through the bamboo floor and anchored itself into a pre-drilled hole. There must have been at least twenty of them. Daniel watched in curiosity as the top section of each bamboo battle tower was lowered, and a large harpoon crossbow was pushed through.

Daniel looked overhead to check the position of the sun. It was almost noon, and still no word on Yuka or Clara. He cast his gaze across the deck when something bobbed up against the hull of his ship. Buffalos swiveled their harpoons to starboard and waited with bated breath, but nothing erupted from the waters.

The Guardian Buffalo tapped his hooves against the deck, and Daniel turned to his right.

"False alarm, Emperor Warrior Nguyen," said the Guardian Buffalo in a low voice.

"What are we looking for?" asked Daniel.

With a pause, the Guardian Buffalo simply said, "The cranes call them the *Ikuchi*, we simply called them sea serpents."

* * *

Clara sat on the ground. She was thankful to be back on dirt. How she longed to be on solid dirt, instead of the sterile desolation of The Shards. With her quiver on her back, the Bow of Destiny laid down beside her, and her knees raised up, she stared at Yuka, who was leaning against the Longevity Tree and seemed to be peacefully asleep. A couple of hours had passed, and she hadn't seen any falling golden leaf.

The only disturbance came when the two cranes who had previously peeled off toward Crane Castle had returned. Atop of one was a rabbit herbalist, who quickly hopped off the crane with a bamboo container strapped to her back: She would be the one to prepare the golden leaf and administer it to Yuka, should one fall.

As the Guardian Panda waited with the Guardian Crane, the four other cranes positioned themselves around the tree to keep vigil for the elusive falling golden leaf. Clara decided to sit by herself, watching Yuka. She felt hopeless as time went on and had no idea if Yuka was already in contact with the tree on some subconscious level. She didn't know if Yuka's experience would be similar to what she went through in the Jade Labyrinth. But Yuka was the most in tune with her Asian heritage. She was fluent in both speaking and writing Japanese. If the Longevity Tree were to judge her on her authenticity, Yuka should soar above her fellow warriors.

But time was passing, and though Clara was still angry with Daniel, she was worried for him and Sung. For all she knew, Sung and Daniel were already engaged in the third battle with the Warlock's army. Though the crane and panda armies would be there, they were handicapped without the protection of their jades. Clara could only hope for the best as she momentarily closed her eyes to the darkness.

***

Darkness was all Yuka could see. She ran in all directions, but never reached an end or a beginning. But while in darkness, she saw that she was strangely aglow in an iridescent blue aura. Strangely, she didn't fear it.

"Where am I?" she asked in Japanese, *"Koko wa doko?"*

"Am I dead? *"Watashi wa shinde imasu ka?"*

"Where is everyone?" *"Min'na doko ni iru no?"*

But no answers came back from the void, and though she should have been frustrated, she was not. Whatever place this was, there was a strange tranquility to its darkness. Hopelessly, she sat down, cross legged. She thought back to her last memory before Clara flew off on the Guardian Crane. Clara had simply said, "Remain true."

Yuka nodded and repeated it under her breath in Japanese, "*Sonomama de ite.*"

Suddenly, streaks of blue light radiated out in all directions from underneath her. As she jumped up, the streaks of blue raced outward into the darkness and disappeared.

With wide eyes, her mouth slightly agape and her clenched hands at her chin, she looked around and uttered again, "*Sonomama de ite.*"

Blue streaks of light radiated out from underneath her feet and she looked on with fascination. But this time, the streaks scattered about her and coalesced into a single spot of squiggly lines. Curious, Yuka briskly walked over to the blue lights, but before she could reach them, they soared upward. Yuka stopped in her tracks and watched in awe as the blue streaks exploded into a choreography of beautiful dazzling lines. The darkness started to glow in a shade of blue when finally, Yuka realized what she was seeing: a large tree.

Yuka could only utter *beautiful* in Japanese: "*utsukushī.*"

Soon the tree was in its full glory. The luminescence from the tree brightened the void. Yuka walked slowly around its thick trunk, watching pulsating blue streaks moving through the trunk, the branches and into the glistening leaves themselves.

Yuka realized in astonishment that she was looking at the Qi of the tree! The tree had its own lifeforce, and somehow, the tree was letting her see it. She was in awe of the white beads of light traversing the branching network of Qi channels. But she didn't know why she was seeing it. She looked around aimlessly into the black void.

Her head spun back from the void when she caught out of the corner of her eye something sprouting from the surface. Two roots, about the width of her thigh and four feet apart shot out from the ground and silently reached upward. When they were about eight feet tall, the roots tapered and reached out to each other until they intertwined at the top, forming an arch.

Soon, a shimmering sheet of iridescent blue water started to rise from the ground between the two roots. As it rose, Yuka saw her shoes reflected in the shimmering water. The reflection flowed up her pants. The hem of her top came into view, then her chest, her arms, and when her head was reflected, she gasped.

With her hands over her mouth, she was horrified to see what stared back at her. She had expected to see her face, but what she saw instead was a contorted network of horribly disfigured Qi channels. There were voids in her head, and other clumps of her Qi within her head were flickering. She knew what she had to do. She pulled apart the side flap of her tunic. Fear welled up within her as she nervously let the tunic top drop from her shoulders onto the ground. Without looking at her reflection, she untied the knot around her pants and let them gently drop around her ankles. She stared at her iridescent garments before she reluctantly looked up.

Her eyes filled with tears as a horrifying image stared back at her. The Qi channels along her limbs were flickering, but her core was almost devoid of Qi. She could see the shriveled up Qi channels and aside from pockets of Qi near her heart, her Qi was in disarray.

Yuka fell to her knees and sobbed into her hands as she thought to herself, *I'm broken inside*, as she mumbled in Japanese the same, "*Watashi wa kowarete imasu ka.*"

She felt her chest heaving as she choked back her emotions and wondered what had happened to her. The horrors of her ordeal came back as she felt the tree's tendrils reach inside of her. She felt the air being ripped from her lungs as her eyes strained, feeling like they were about to burst. When she thought she could no longer endure any more agony, the ten searing cups forcefully sucked up her skin as they violently siphoned out her Qi. And when she thought her body could offer nothing more, the Warlock had ordered her to be gutted by the Harvester tree. The Warlock had defiled her and broken her to the point of emptiness. Maybe it would have been better if he had finished the bloody task so that she would not have to live with such dishonor.

As Yuka wept into her hands, the shimmering reflection receded back into the ground, followed by the untwining of the roots.

Yuka didn't know how much time had passed. As she cried with her body hunched over, her iridescent naked body glowed. When she could cry no longer, she covered herself with one arm as she wiped her tears and runny nose, though there were no real tears or mucus in the strange void. She calmed herself, and her hopelessness and despair were soon replaced with seething contempt for the Warlock. The thought of his selfishness, his arrogance, his disregard for life on Azen, and his nefarious hubris coiled up into a single point of emotion, that she let out in a contemptuous scream that reverberated through the void. Her scream shook even the leaves of the bluish Longevity Tree.

Yuka's shoulders drooped and though she didn't feel cold, she thought she should be. She carefully draped her tunic across her shoulders. She grabbed the top of her pants and as she rose, they rose along her legs. Her hands fastened the knot and soon she secured the flap of her tunic at her side. Her eyes were downcast as she brushed down the tunic that now hid her broken Qi. *What was she to do,* she thought? *Was she dying and the place that she was in was that interim place before one's Qi disintegrates, and their soul dissipates into the void?*

But it wasn't what she wanted to happen. She knew she had duties to fulfil, with or without the Qi. She thought about Sung, Daniel, their guardians, the tigers, and the buffalos. Her thoughts wandered to the Guardian Panda and then to Clara, which made her smile. But her final thought focused on the Guardian Crane. She was so fond of her Guardian Crane that despite her fleeting happiness, a tear slowly seeped out of her eye and onto the ground. It splashed apart in a strange bluish glow before it was absorbed into the blackness.

Suddenly, on the ground, an iridescent bluish square materialized. Yuka looked down and knelt in front of it. Her hand reached for it and as she picked it up, she realized it was a stiff piece of paper. Despite only its edges glowing, it was not transparent as she thought it would be. She flipped it over, and only blackness stared back at her.

Yuka looked up at the tree, perplexed. She held out the piece of paper and said *I don't understand,* in Japanese: *"Wakaranai."*

The only response was silence. She held the square piece of paper in both hands, wondering what was in her last thoughts to trigger the appearance of the piece of paper. *Her Guardian Crane was her last thought,* she realized. A grin spread across her face: She realized what the paper was.

She quickly placed the paper on the ground and started to fold it. As each fold creased, a bluish line appeared. A bend there. A tuck there, and soon, she raised in her hand an origami crane. She chuckled as she stared at the modest *origami* crane when suddenly, it glistened. Yuka's eyes stared as its head moved, and she let out a gasp. Its wings fluttered, and the *origami* crane lifted off into the air as Yuka gasped in awe. The *origami* crane found a branch and settled onto it.

Happiness began to fill the void in Yuka's soul as she brought her feet and hands together and stood up straight. She bowed respectfully to the crane as she uttered, *Good luck to you*, in Japanese, "*Ganbatte!*"

Yuka's expression turned to wonderment when suddenly at her feet, multiple pieces of paper appeared. But not just ones with the iridescent blue edges, but others in glowing purple, red, and yellow. She knelt and looked about her as she thought there was easily a hundred pieces of paper. She playfully picked up another piece of *origami* paper and quickly folded that into a crane, which too fluttered upward to another branch.

Her mind and hands were one as she folded another *origami* crane, which also fluttered upward. Her smile grew wider with each one. Her hands did not tire, and she simply picked up the next piece of *origami* paper, folded it with glee, and allowed it to flutter upward. In time, hundreds of *origami* cranes were nestled in the branches of the Longevity Tree. Their wings fluttered lightly as they watched Yuka tirelessly fold more of their brethren.

Yuka reached out to the yellow-edged *origami* paper and paused. She looked about her and saw there were no more pieces of *origami* paper on the ground. She let out a sigh and carefully folded her last *origami* crane. She held it in her hand and smiled as it came to life. But unlike the others, it didn't flutter away immediately. It craned its head downward and looked at Yuka. She felt a sudden fondness for the last *origami* crane and brought it closer to her and smiled at it. With a gentle voice, she said *fly* in Japanese, "*tobu*." She extended out her hands. The reluctant crane looked upward and flew away, into the branches of the Longevity Tree and settled onto a branch.

Yuka brought her hands down into her lap and realized that as she was folding, all the hopelessness and despair she had been feeling had been lifted away. Reflected in her eyes were the shimmering of one thousand blue, purple, red, and yellow *origami* cranes.

She let out *beautiful*, in Japanese, "*utsukushī*."

The light darkened as the void slowly collapsed in on itself.

* * *

"The battle must have commenced by now," said the Guardian Panda to the Guardian Crane.

The Guardian Crane nodded. "I'm afraid as much. How do you think they are faring?"

"Not well as we're not there," said the Guardian Panda. "We have been patient long enough. Perhaps I'll take Empress Warrior Wu with me to the battlefront to bolster the panda army. Our panda archers are good with their bows, but they can always use the support from the Bamboo Jade."

The Guardian Crane nodded reluctantly, "Yes, I think you're right. I'll stay with Empress Warrior Satoh and hope…"

"There!" screamed an excited Clara who picked up her bow and excitedly pointed to the Longevity Tree. "A leaf fell! I saw it!"

Without another word, the Guardian Crane flew to Clara, who mounted the Guardian Crane as the Guardian Panda mounted Shiori. As Himari the rabbit herbalist prepared to receive the lone golden leaf, two cranes raced across the Healing Pool to the island of the Longevity Tree.

The Guardian Crane skimmed the pool's watery surface until its talons brushed the ground as Clara yelled, "There! I see it!"

The Guardian Crane landed, and Clara hopped off with a thud. She briskly ran to the golden leaf that had fallen to the ground and stared at it for a moment. It was a perfect oval leaf with a stem, and when Clara picked it up, she realized it was thin, like tin foil.

"Tuck it carefully into your chest, Empress Warrior Wu," exclaimed the Guardian Crane.

Clara nodded and carefully nestled it behind her chest plate. She turned around and saw that the Guardian Panda held Yuka, still listless, in his arms. The Guardian Crane leaned slightly to her side to allow Clara to easily jump aboard. Clara quickly gripped the harness and reached down toward the Guardian Panda. She pulled Yuka up and cradled her. With one hand on the harness, she let out, "Go!"

The Guardian Crane wasted no time flying the short distance across the Healing Pool to land by the awaiting rabbit. Yuka murmured as Clara placed her chin on top of Yuka's head. Soon, the Guardian Panda landed and rushed to Clara, allowing her to transfer Yuka into his strong, black furry arms. He gently placed Yuka face up on the tatami mat and knelt by her head. Clara dismounted from the Guardian Crane.

Clara reached into her chest plate and carefully pulled out the golden leaf. With trembling hands, she quickly handed it to the eager rabbit, who took it in both of her paws as the Guardian Crane circled to her side. The other three cranes flew in, surrounded the group and stood guard.

Clara sat by Yuka's right shoulder, rubbing Yuka's clammy hand to impart some of her warmth. She watched with curiosity as Himari inspected the golden leaf. Holding it gently in both of her paws, she bowed to it before letting it drop into a stone mortar. All the tools were laid out perfectly as she picked up the stone pestle. With gentle swirls, she ground the leaf into a fine golden powder. She placed the pestle down and transferred the fine golden powder into a folded piece of paper. Her paw came upon the metal handle of a tea kettle that was atop a small burning element. With a deft movement of her two paws, she carefully poured hot water into another clay bowl and placed the tea kettle back onto the burning element. The golden dust was then poured into the bowl of hot water. With a bamboo whisk, she carefully stirred its contents until the golden dust slowly dissolved. She quickly covered the clay bowl with its lid and let it seep for a minute. With care, she placed the heated clay bowl into a larger bowl of cool water. After a minute, she took it out, wiped it dry with a ceremonial cloth, and moved toward Yuka's head.

The Guardian Panda gently tilted back Yuka's head as Clara parted Yuka's lips. Himari slowly poured the golden elixir into Yuka's mouth, pausing to let her swallow, then pouring again until there was no more.

The rabbit pulled her paws back as the Guardian Crane looked closer. The Guardian Panda placed Yuka's head back on the tatami mat. Clara looked up and exclaimed, "I think it's working!"

The Guardian Crane asked, "How do you know, Empress Warrior Wu?"

Clara rubbed Yuka's hand with both of her hands and could feel a gradual warmth. "Her hand, it's much warmer now…"

Just then, golden streaks of light flashed along Yuka's right hand and fingers. Her left hand also showed similar streaks of light underneath her skin. Yuka murmured and tilted her head back as her whole face illuminated in a golden flash. The flashes suddenly appeared everywhere and glowed underneath her clothing around her chest, stomach, thighs, shins, feet until finally, all the flashes coalesced into one final bright glow.

When Clara's eyes readjusted from the unexpected glow, she heard Yuka's voice, "Where am I?"

Clara looked down at a bewildered Yuka as she looked at her.

"Yuka!" screamed Clara with joy as Yuka's eyes shifted to the Guardian Crane.

"Guardian Crane," said Yuka whose eyes shifted upward toward the Guardian Panda. "Guardian Panda, and hello, who might you be?"

"Empress Warrior Satoh," said the rabbit herbalist respectfully. "I'm Hirami, the Crane Kingdom's top herbalist."

Yuka pushed herself up, and the Guardian Panda helped her into a sitting position. Yuka shook her head lightly as she took in a deep breath before looking back up at everyone.

"How do you feel?" asked Clara.

Yuka smiled and placed her left hand over Clara's warm hands. "Better. I feel better. Great battle armor, Clara!"

Clara laughed at Yuka's unexpected cheeriness while looking fondly at her.

Yuka turned to the Longevity Tree, sensing something familiar about it, "I know that tree, don't I?"

"Yes, Empress Warrior Satoh," said the Guardian Crane. "That is the Longevity Tree. It saved your life."

Yuka smiled as the memories flooded back into her. She bowed slightly toward the tree and uttered *Thank you for saving my life*, in Japanese, "*Watashi no inochi wo tasukute kurete arigatō.*"

"Empress Warrior Wu," beckoned the Guardian Crane as Clara looked up. "The Moon Star *shuriken.*"

Clara nodded and reached into her chest plate and pulled out the Moon Star *shuriken* with its dim white jade. Yuka extended her hand and Clara looked up at her.

"Don't worry," said Yuka calmly. "It'll be fine."

Clara passed the Moon Star to Yuka, who gingerly held the two opposing points and glanced down at it. She looked up at the Guardian Crane with a grin.

"All is fine," said Yuka as she placed her thumb on the white jade. In an instant, a bead of white light spiraled out of the white jade and blasted out. As it did, the white jade embedded in the black mesh body suit of the Guardian Crane was lit aglow, and she let out a sigh. She turned to the other four cranes and saw that they were gawking at each other's glowing white jades. The Guardian Crane knew that Yuka's Qi had been restored by the Longevity Tree.

"Our mission is done," began the Guardian Crane. "Guardian Panda, you and Empress Warrior Wu will go to the battlefront along with the other two Top Talon cranes. I will return Empress Warrior Satoh back to the safety of Crane Castle…"

"No!" Yuka protested, catching everyone by surprise. "I can go, the cranes need the power of the jade."

"Empress Warrior Satoh," the Guardian Crane beseeched. "You have just been through a tortuous ordeal…"

"Guardian Crane," said Yuka firmly. "Please forgive me, I mean no disrespect. You saved me, now I must save the cranes!"

The beady eyes of the Guardian Crane looked straight at the respectfully defiant Crane Warrior before she looked at the Guardian Panda, Clara, Hirami and simply said *ascend* in Japanese: "*jōshō suru!*"

TWENTY - TWO

Daniel took a few startled steps backward as the hulking girth of the silverish sea serpent reared upward from the starboard side and arced over the battle vessel. Its scales glistened in the sunlight as it loomed over even the tallest mast, just barely escaping the sharp curved blades set atop it. A slick ooze dripped from its body and onto the wooden deck, rendering it precariously slippery.

But the sea buffalos were prepared. They had donned oil-slicked gear, which allowed the sticky ooze to slide off them and onto the deck. With steady hooves, the buffalos swept the deck with large brooms to push off the serpent ooze.

As the sea serpent completed its descent over the port side, Daniel guessed that it was at least one hundred feet in length. But what caught his attention was the large wooden sphere cradled in its tail. The buffalos aimed their harpoon crossbows at the sea serpent, and two harpoons hit their mark as a ghoulish shriek rang out. As the sea serpent disappeared into the water, the slack on the tether lines spiraled out of their coils on the deck with blistering speed. The other end of the tether line was attached to a large metal crossbar with a shorter crossbar in the center. The forty-foot crossbar was hoisted up by the buffalos just as two large eagles flew in and gripped the top of the crossbar. They flew upwards as two other eagles flew in and grasped the middle crossbar, flapping strenuously in unison until the tether snapped taut. The sea serpent wailed against its restraints and thrashed in the water until finally, with a flick of its large tail, it tossed the wooden sphere into the air. It flew a mighty distance before splashing down into the water near the coastline, where it simply floated. But moments later, the wooden sphere started splashing toward the beach.

"Emperor Warrior Nguyen," commanded the Guardian Buffalo. "Light those wooden spheres ablaze!"

Daniel nodded and invoked a thrust Qi element, and as he lifted off, the ocean came alive as dozens of sea serpents arced over all the battle vessels. The air was loud with the zinging of harpoons, the thrashing of water, the flapping of eagle wings, heavy grunts from the buffalos, and the frantic squawking of eagles.

Daniel flew to the first wooden sphere and hit it with a fireball, which was rendered useless as the sphere rolled over into the water. He turned around, and the entire ocean before him was a swarm of harpooned sea serpents, thrashing wildly in the water. Many of the eagles were forced to let go of their metal crossbars as the sea serpents were too strong. The sea serpents simply dove into the water, but with tens of sea serpents in the same body of water, the tethers that had been harpooned into them tangled together beneath the waters as the clunky crossbars sank to the bottom, acting as clumsy anchors.

Though the sea serpents were mired in chaos, they managed to toss dozens of wooden spheres toward the beach, where they floated ominously. Daniel did his best to hit each one with a fireball, but these were immediately extinguished as the spheres splashed forward. Daniel quickly adapted and started to hit the spheres on the sides. This forced the mysterious creatures inside to shift their direction to push the burning side of the sphere into the water. But while this slowed them down, it didn't stop them. There were simply too many, and they were still too far from shore for the pandas' arrows to reach them.

Daniel's attention suddenly turned to one of the vessels. One of the sea serpents had gotten caught in the menacing curved blade, causing it to collapse onto the deck of one of the battle vessels. As it writhed on the deck, it wrought havoc as its body coiled around the entire ship, bringing the metal net up with it and crushing the wooden hull and forcing it to take on water.

But to his horror, Daniel soon saw a second wave of sea serpents sneaking through the breach in the barricade. They broke the surface and navigated through the first wave of entangled sea serpents. The tails of the second wave of sea serpents broke through the surface as they flung their wooden spheres through the air. Daniel thrusted out of their way and blasted as many as he could with fireballs.

On the beach, Sung stood next to Hanro, the Head of the Prowlers, who was watching the mayhem in the water. The blockade had stalled the massive sea serpents, which were the largest creatures he had ever seen. But he was glad that they were being ensnared in the harpoon tethers and thrashing amongst themselves. Still, the hundreds of wooden spheres and their enigmatic cargo that were barreling toward the shore were worrisome to Sung.

"Are you ready, Emperor Warrior Kim?" asked Hanro.

"Yes, Hanro," said Sung. "What should I do?"

"Freeze the water," Hanro said.

With a nod, Sung invoked an ice bridge and soared into the air. At some fifty feet up, he could see the carnage. He saw Daniel frantically launching fireballs at as many wooden spheres as possible. Sung invoked an ice Qi element and froze the water below, creating an ice sheet. He invoked a few more but suddenly saw a misjudgment as the wooden spheres simply skipped out of the water and onto the ice sheet. Abetted by the slippery ice sheet, the wooden spheres rolled effortlessly toward the beach. Then they stopped.

Sung's eyes focused on the wooden spheres, which simply lay on the beach. The panda archers launched their fire tipped arrows, and sent them into the wooden spheres. But as the wooden spheres burst into flames, doors at the back of the wooden spheres flung open. Gruesome humanoid creatures burst out, emitting loud grunts as they raced up the beach with shields, clubs, swords, maces, spears, and *surujins*, lengths of rope that were weighted at both ends.

Hanro, with his whiskers fluttering in the breeze, looked over to his Prowlers and muttered, "*Oni*"—*ogre* in Japanese. The first wave of the brutish *oni* were met with arrows from the panda archers, but the *onis* did not fall easily. Instead, they simply ripped the arrows from their flesh and continued onward. Their tenacious strength was going to be tough to fight. The battle buffalos and tigers rushed and leapt into action to meet the oncoming *onis*, who lumbered forward, fighting in a clumsy but brutishly coordinated manner. Using shields and spears, they held their own against the battle buffalos and tigers.

Sung turned back to a crashing sound and saw that the ice sheet he had created was being battered from below by sea serpents. They could only get so close to shore in shallow water, but when possible, they picked up any wayward wooden sphere near them and threw it the rest of the way toward the beach. Sung grew frustrated as he tried to refocus, erecting ice walls to slow down the spheres. But the crowd of sea serpents near the shoreline were breaking up his ice sheets.

Daniel could see gaps in the blockade as scores of wooden spheres rolled through. The giant sea serpents that had managed to get through unscathed were pulling out the harpoons embedded in the other sea serpents. Once freed, they relentlessly flung their wooden spheres toward the beach.

The battlefront was alive with shrieks and calls from the eagles and cranes who were diving valiantly to slice through the scaled armor of the sea serpents breaking through the surface. But several of the cranes were slammed by the sea serpents' bodies as they came crashing back into the water.

The beachhead was in mayhem as buffalos clad in full armor rammed into scores of *onis*, who simply got back up. They seemed invincible despite the bloody gashes that had penetrated their leathered armor. Arrows sang through the air, but the frenzied movement of the *onis* caused many of the arrows to go astray.

Soaring over the bamboo battle towers were five large eagles. Their massive wingspans cast large shadows, causing the battle pandas to look up. The Guardian Tiger peered over the shoulder of his eagle and saw how the battle tigers and buffalos were struggling against the *onis*. Their battle along the northern front was failing, so he growled *charge* ferociously in Korean: "*Gong gyuck!*"

In an instant, the Guardian Tiger and the exhausted but battle-hungry Prowlers from the rescue mission leapt off the mighty eagles and into the bloody fray of battle.

TWENTY - THREE

Daniel soared away from the snapping jaws of a sea serpent before its weight sent it crashing back into the water below. The waters were teeming with sea serpents entangled in tether lines with cranes and eagles struggling to pull on the metal crossbars at the other end. At the same time, the cranes and eagles were trying to avoid being snapped up by the jaws of the sea serpents that breached the water. But some of the winged warriors were not so fortunate and were torn asunder, leaving their mangled feathery bodies to crash into the waters. Fast-moving schooners skimmed the perimeter, trying to harpoon the sea serpents. There were hits but mainly misses, and when they did hit, the screeches from the sea serpents were riveting as they dove back into the water.

In the mayhem, more wooden spheres were still rolling toward the beach, their progress slowed by Sung's ice sheets and walls. But these barriers couldn't stop the *onis* from erupting from the wooden spheres and dashing on foot toward the beach. Daniel blasted the wooden spheres marooned in the ice sheet with fireballs. Some sank into the water, but to Daniel's dismay, several *onis* rose to the surface and even swam toward the ice sheet before continuing their advance.

Daniel shot a look at the ferocious battles being fought at the beach. The buffalos were ramming the *onis* at will, but some succumbed as *onis* overwhelmed them. The agile tigers slashed, sending crimson ribbons into the air. Arrows from the pandas zinged through the air, some hitting their marks while others missed. But the bamboo towers were still quiet: The large crossbows were not being deployed, and Daniel wondered why.

Sung suddenly soared up to Daniel, balanced precariously atop an almost vertical ice column, with the Claw Staff strapped to the back of his battle armor. He looked exhausted as he looked down at the mayhem.

"I'm almost out of my Qi elements," said Sung. "I can feel it. Not a whole lot of good that snow can do here."

Daniel invoked another thrust Qi element, but he too felt spent. Before he could respond to Sung, he watched Sung's expression turn to shock as he started to fall downward as the impact of a sea serpent's tail shattered the base of the ice bridge.

Daniel shot downward, stretched out his right hand and grabbed Sung's right hand firmly, holding him in midair. Sung let out a sigh and looked up at Daniel. "You can let go. I got it from here."

Daniel looked at him and replied, "Sure?"

"Yep," said Sung.

Daniel grinned and let his friend go. As Sung fell straight down, he invoked a column Qi element. An ice column rose from the waters to meet his feet. He landed on top of the column of ice with a thud, quickly invoked a bridge Qi element, and surfed back toward the beach. Along the way, he invoked more ice walls to frustrate the oncoming *onis* and wooden spheres.

Daniel soared away from a snapping sea serpent and sent a fireball at its head before it sank beneath the surface of the water. His eyes widened as he saw a new problem: The *onis* were climbing up the tether lines toward the cranes and eagles. The winged warriors were battling exhaustion as they struggled to hold the sea serpents at bay. Flying cranes who saw the danger flew in closer to their kin and sliced through the *onis* with their *katana* wings. *Oni* halves toppled into the crimson ocean. But despite the aviators' valiant attempts, they were tiring, and for whatever reason, the sea serpents and the *onis* were not.

Daniel flew in close and knocked off the threatening *onis* with his fireballs. He flew toward another tether with three *onis* climbing stubbornly upward. He invoked a fireball Qi element, but nothing happened. He looked at his hand and tried again: nothing. He had depleted all his fireball Qi elements. Daniel flew off a bit, daring not to use a stream Qi element as it could singe the tether.

Despite his exhaustion, he inhaled deeply as he brought forth the club horn and gritted his teeth. He thrusted off and soared in close and could finally see how gnarly the *onis'* muscles were. When he saw the distorted face of the *oni* looking at him, he clubbed its head. The blow sent it reeling away from the tether as it plummeted toward the chaotic waters beneath. Daniel flew to another tether with two *onis*, and he clubbed the first one and circled back and knocked off the second one.

Daniel soared upward, his breath labored, and looked down at the glowing red jade atop the club. He needed to fight on, though he felt overwhelmed by the battle. He knew that Sung was fighting valiantly along the shoreline, all by himself. He realized that two Azen warriors were simply not enough to take on an entire Warlock army, especially one as unrelentingly strong as the sea serpents and *onis*.

The excited calls of the cranes around him caught his attention, and he looked up to see the flying bellies of five cranes. They whizzed by with determination, and though Daniel could only see their underbellies, he knew it was the rescue squadron. They flew away toward the tallest limestone rock as the lead crane gracefully landed. He knew in his gut that it was the Guardian Crane! When she folded her wings inward, there were two figures straddling her.

Daniel's heavy heart suddenly lifted. *It had to be Clara and Yuka!* Yuka had been successfully rescued, and the heavy weight on his heart was lifted. He wanted to thrust over to them, but he was hesitant. He didn't know how Clara would receive him considering she'd been angry enough to slap him across the face. But who he really worried about was Yuka and whether or not she would forgive him.

The shrill call of a crane nearby stole Daniel's attention as he saw an *oni* within reach of the crossbar. He snapped from his thoughts to strike the offending *oni*.

Clara jumped off the Guardian Crane and unslung her bow. She glanced out at the bloody icy carnage in the waters. The other four Top Talon cranes settled roughly along the four corners atop the tallest limestone rock and acted as sentries. Clara reached upward toward a weakened but able Yuka and carefully guided her down onto the limestone surface.

Yuka smiled at Clara, her left arm draped across Clara's shoulders as Clara's right arm wrapped around Yuka's waist for support. Together, they took a few steps toward the edge with the Guardian Crane alongside them.

For the first time, Yuka took in the bloody sea carnage. Sea serpents thrashed and battled with the Buffalo Kingdom's battle vessels, the exhausted winged warriors pulled on the tethers, and the beach in the distance was thrashing in crimson mayhem.

Yuka produced the Moon Star from her top and looked at Clara. She scanned the top of the limestone rocks around her, where hundreds of idled cranes all stared at her and Clara.

"Ready to do this?" asked Clara.

Yuka looked back at Clara and nodded. She looked straight ahead and from somewhere within her exhausted body, she mustered the strength to call out to the red crowned cranes in Japanese, *"Tanchō! Washi."* With all beady eyes on her, she raised the Moon Star into the air as she slid her thumb across its white jade. A brilliant flash of light spiraled outward and vanished in a blink of an eye. She yelled out with authority, *dive!* in Japanese, "*tsukkome!*"

The cacophony of excited shrieks erupted from the hundreds of cranes and eagles as they saw their white jades glowing on their meshed body armor. Following Yuka's lead, Clara raised the Bow of Destiny into the air as the same white light radiated out from the Bamboo Jade, reactivating all the green jades on the pandas' bamboo armor and arrow tips.

Yuka leaned into Clara and watched as hundreds of cranes and eagles, with renewed energy and hope, dove down into the watery fracas to join the battle.

TWENTY - FOUR

"Bring out the jade harpoons now!" ordered a weary Guardian Buffalo as the sea buffalos rolled out huge green bamboo containers. It took two buffalos to twist off the bamboo cap to reveal the vertically stored harpoons. The bottom half of each harpoon tip was Clawdium, but the top half was topped off with a glowing green jade. The regular metal harpoons were pulled out of the crossbows as the jade-tipped harpoons were eagerly loaded. All the harpoons across the ships spun in synchrony as metal gears cranked and the sea buffalos looked through the sights.

At the beach, Sung was distracted by a flurry of activity in the bamboo battle towers. With his troops' morale boosted by the glowing green jade on their battle armor, the panda in charge of the battle towers ordered his pandas to load the crossbows with the heavy jade-tipped arrows. Each one was loaded with a deliberate thud, and the panda at the trigger in back swiveled the crossbow and targeted the sea serpents by the shoreline.

In silent harmony, the sea buffalos and pandas let loose the jade-tipped harpoons and arrows with a tether trailing each one. Each green jade tip found its mark as it pierced the scales of a sea serpent. As each harpoon and heavy arrow sank into the sea serpents' flesh, flanges opened when tugged on, painfully lodging themselves into the sea serpents' flesh as they shrieked in agony.

From within the battle towers, the strongest of the pandas started to grind away at the winch attached to the other end of the tethers. The tethers grew taut across all the bamboo battle towers as the sea serpents writhed against them. Entire walls of the bamboo tower shook against the force of the sea serpents' strength, but the pandas kept turning the winches until finally, one by one, each sea serpent was pulled across buckled ice sheets onto the sandy beaches. Panda archers let loose a volley of jade-tipped arrows, which sunk through their scaly armor.

The sea serpents near the blockade fared no better: They were hoisted into the air by the powerful eagles. As they struggled to free themselves from the deeply embedded harpoons, scores of cranes sliced through them with their *katana* wings, slashing them with a thousand cuts.

Determined cranes who had previously sat out most of the battle now flew energetically toward the ice sheets and halved the remaining *onis*. Along the beach, the panda archers switched to their jade-tipped arrows and took out the remaining *onis* effortlessly.

With all the wooden spheres already launched, the sea serpents who had worked themselves free of the harpoons or remained uninjured dove beneath the water's surface. They slithered away as they meandered past the sunken bodies of *onis* and their bloodied brethren. They slithered toward the gaps in the naval blockade as the bottoms of the schooners skimmed the water from above. With their nostrils flaring and gray eyes bulging, they navigated between the watery clanging of metal nets dangling from the bellies of the battle vessels that were forced to break formation. They soon passed through the gaps toward open water. Soon the blood-drenched water was behind them.

As the surviving sea serpents breached the water beyond the watery battlefront, they glided along the surface in defeat. In front of them was an even bigger sea serpent that was just idling in the water. It stared at the retreating serpents with its black eyes as they sailed passed.

The lone sea serpent floated motionless atop the water. Its large snake-like head breached the surface as its watery eyes stared ahead. Atop its scaly head stood a large *oni*, who was staring ahead. He was expressionless, and knew the battle was lost. Besides reporting to the Warlock of the loss, he would have the dreaded obligation to inform the Warlock that the Air Wu Warrior had returned safely to Azen.

He tugged on the rope harness tied behind the sea serpent's head. It silently spun around in the water and slithered away.

TWENTY - FIVE

A hand placed a round black pebble onto a board with a black grid. Then a beak placed a white pebble onto the board. Another black one came onto the board, followed by another white one right after. Then a black one and finally a white one.

"You beat me again!" exclaimed Yuka with a giggle, looking up at the young crane at the foot of her bed as they played the popular Japanese pebble game *go*. The young crane fluttered his feathers with giddiness and squealed with glee. He leveled his gaze at Yuka and smiled.

"Well, I have been playing *go* for a long time, Empress Warrior Satoh," he said with humility. "Would you like to play again?"

Yuka brought her hands up as the soft blanket about her waist ruffled. She was about to reach for the pebbles when a knock came from her door at Crane Castle.

Both Yuka and the young crane turned their heads as the Guardian Crane entered with a smile.

"Aki, are you having fun with Empress Warrior Satoh?" asked the Guardian Crane of her son.

Aki turned to his mother, the Guardian Crane, and blurted out in excitement. "It's very fun! We played ten games of *go*! We were about to play another game."

Yuka grinned from cheek to cheek at Aki's excitement.

"Ten games are enough. Let's let Empress Warrior Satoh rest, okay?" asked the Guardian Crane as she looked sternly at her young son.

Aki's beak slumped as he swiveled toward Yuka.

"Empress Warrior Satoh," said Aki. "It was an honor to play *go* with you and I hope we can play again soon!"

Yuka brought her hands together along with a smile, "Of course we can, Aki! When I return next time, I promise."

Aki smiled and quickly lowered his head to fold the *go* board in half as the sound of pebbles gently scraped the wooden board, which formed its own box. Aki flicked a latch to lock it shut and flipped up an embedded handle.

"Have a good day, Empress Warrior Satoh," said Aki cheerfully as he picked up the handle of the *go* board with his beak and turned toward the door. He bowed to his mother. When he got to the sliding door, his beady eyes widened before exiting as the door slid shut.

"I had so much fun meeting and playing with your son!" exclaimed Yuka as she turned slightly toward the Guardian Crane.

The Guardian Crane smiled and looking down at Yuka, asked, "And how do you feel after a full night's rest?"

Yuka paused, looked down as she clasped her hands in front of her. Despite the horrible tortuous memories that would forever be seared into her mind, the Longevity Tree had restored her, and she could feel it. She couldn't explain it, but she just knew intuitively that she was fine.

She looked back up at the Guardian Crane and simply said, "I'm whole again. I can feel it."

"I'm glad to hear that, Empress Warrior Satoh," said the Guardian Crane. "The Longevity Tree has great healing powers."

"Mmmm," said Yuka in agreement.

"If you will give me a moment, Empress Warrior Satoh," said the Guardian Crane as she stepped back toward the door. "The others would like to see you now."

The Guardian Crane gently tapped on the door, and it slid open as Yuka's eyes lit up. Clara, smiling in a spring-themed top and bamboo-colored pants, bounded in. Clara rushed toward Yuka and threw her arms around her as Yuka hugged her back. She nestled her chin into Clara's neck as a tear of gratitude fell from her eye.

"Hey Yuka!" said Sung, who waltzed in nonchalantly in a slick short robe over a fitted top and tapered pants.

Clara pulled back and turned around. Yuka smiled heartily. She had not seen Sung since she flew to the Warlock's fortress. Not even at the end of sea battle did she see anyone else, as she had been immediately flown back to Crane Castle, where Hirami had examined her fully.

Yuka eagerly reached toward Sung, who gave Yuka a warm embrace. As she did, Daniel walked cautiously into the room. He was wearing a longer robe, a loose top, and straight pants.

"Hi Yuka," said Daniel cautiously.

Yuka's friendly demeanor changed as she looked up at Daniel, expressionless. As Sung pulled away, Yuka weakly waved at Daniel. With an awkward chuckle, Daniel moved in and placed his arms awkwardly upon Yuka's shoulders. Yuka's expression of discomfort was only exacerbated by her halfhearted pat on Daniel's back.

He pulled away, showing his somewhat lanky demeanor for the first time, and collected himself. He looked down at Yuka and pointed, "Hey, you look great. Like almost nothing happened."

Yuka glared and uttered a grunt of displeasure.

"Hey, what's wrong?" asked Daniel.

Sung stood up and uttered, "Dude, that's not cool."

Daniel glared at him defensively. "Hey, she's okay now. Nothing happened to her in the end."

"Daniel!" screamed Clara. "How can you be so insensitive?"

Daniel looked back at his three friends' expressions, from Yuka's shock, Sung's disbelief, and Clara's contempt.

"It's not my fault!" Daniel shouted as he fled the room in a huff.

As he raced down the hall red faced, Clara grabbed him and spun him around angrily until he was face to face with her.

"What is your problem?!" Clara screamed.

Daniel looked incredulous. "My problem? What's Yuka's problem? She wouldn't have been captured if she hadn't followed me."

"She followed you because she was worried about you!"

"No one forced her to go! She should have just let me go by myself. I would have been fine!"

"You don't know that. You could have been captured, and no one would have known and who knows what the Warlock could have done to you?" Clara retorted.

"What did he do? Huh? Tell me. What did the Warlock do to her? How bad could it have been?"

Clara angrily recapped what she saw when the Guardian Crane barreled into what she called the torture room. How she saw Yuka forcibly held down on the table by sinister branches and how she looked like she was beaten from her torn clothing. How she had just arrived in time as the other tree was about to slice her open to get to her Qi.

Daniel stared at Clara as he tried to absorb what she was telling him. His emotions crumbled as he blurted out, "Oh my god, what did I do?"

Daniel slumped to his knees and sobbed uncontrollably. Through his choked back emotions, he uttered, "I didn't mean for her to be captured. This was all my fault! I wish I was the one to have been captured!"

As mad as Clara was at Daniel, she dropped to her knees in front of him as she pulled him close, allowing him to sob on her shoulder. She held him as he sobbed, his chest heaving at times, until he finally uttered, "I'm sorry."

Clara's face was expressionless as she uttered, "Don't tell me, tell Yuka."

Daniel choked back on his tears and mumbled, "I don't know how. She probably hates me."

Clara rolled her eyes gently, suddenly feeling like an older sister. "She doesn't hate you. Maybe mad at you. But she doesn't hate you."

"Do you think she'll ever forgive me?" Daniel mumbled through his sobs.

"You have to let her forgive you, but you have to earn it first," said Clara as she continued to console him.

TWENTY - SIX

Clara returned to Yuka's quarters after leaving Daniel, who said he needed some fresh air. A crane attendant nodded, and Clara nodded back as the crane gently slid the partition back. Clara stepped through and she could hear Yuka and Sung laughing.

"What's so funny?" asked Clara with a smile. Sung turned to her from his seated position on the edge of the bed. Yuka also looked up with a smile and patted the edge of the bed, beckoning Clara to sit down near her.

Clara skipped over to the bed but before she could sit down, Sung pointed at her shoulder and asked, "Ewe, what's all that gunk on your shoulder?"

Clara stopped in her tracks and looked surprised. She looked at her shoulder, saw a wet gooey mess, and was a bit disgusted by it. But she exhaled, shrugged, and looked at Sung and Yuka.

"Oh, it's nothing," said Clara casually. "Daniel just had an ugly cry."

Sung laughed and said, "You made him ugly cry?"

Clara laughed too, but Yuka looked puzzled as she asked, "What's an ugly cry?"

"Oh, you know," said Sung as he turned to Yuka and imitated an ugly cry with contorted facial features.

Yuka laughed, "Oh, ugly cry, I get it."

"I better go check up on him," said Sung as he rose and Clara and Yuka admired his handsome outfit.

"I think he's out on The Perch," said Clara.

"Got it," said Sung as he waved goodbye. "I'll see you at the Portal Circle tomorrow."

"See ya," said Clara as Yuka said, "*Soyōnara!*"

Sung exited and the partition door slid shut. Clara hopped onto the edge of the bed and Yuka leaned in closer. They clasped each other's hands and smiled at each other. Clara noticed that Yuka's hands were their normal warm selves.

"Are you doing okay?" asked Clara.

"Mm-hmm…" said Yuka with her lips pursed. Despite her tortuous ordeal, there was a certain brightness in her eyes.

"Are you sure?" asked Clara cautiously. "You were really hurt when we rescued you. And the welts on your back looked horrible."

Yuka smiled and gently hushed Clara. She looked around suspiciously as if there were prying eyes. She pushed away her blanket, straightened up and twisted away from Clara. She gently pulled up her top and Clara could see only smooth flawless skin on Yuka's back.

"They're gone!" said Clara incredulously. "Can I?"

Yuka nodded as Clara reached toward her, gliding her fingers gently along Yuka's back, where she remembered seeing the deep purplish-reddish round welts. Nothing seemed amiss as she pulled her hand back in wonderment. Yuka pulled down her top as Clara looked back up at her.

"The Longevity Tree?" said Clara.

"Mm-hmm," said Yuka as she clasped her hands in her lap.

"What did it say to you?" asked Clara.

"It didn't speak to me," said Yuka. "I don't know if it was in my mind, or I was in its mind. But it was dark, and I was glowing in this blue light. Then the Longevity Tree appeared. Well, it wasn't exactly the Longevity Tree, but its Qi, in the shape of itself. It was so beautiful and calming. It created this tall arch with shimmering water, and I could see my reflection. But where my face should be, it wasn't my face. It was my Qi," Yuka paused.

"Then the saddest part. I undressed, and when I looked at my reflection, I could see how my Qi was broken all throughout my body. I didn't know if I was dying or already dead. All I do remember was… ugly cry." Despite the harrowing memory, Yuka chuckled.

"When I could no longer cry, I got dressed. I didn't know what the tree was trying to say to me. I didn't know what to do. But I thought of all of you and of course my Guardian Crane. And that's when I saw it: a square piece of paper on the ground. I picked it up and there was no message. I didn't know what to do and thought back to my last thought, which was the Guardian Crane. Then I realized it was *origami* paper! It was like I suddenly knew what to do and I folded an *origami* crane. And this is the exciting part! It came to life!"

"Whoa!" exclaimed Clara. "What did it do?"

"It flew away onto one of the branches, and when I looked down, I saw more *origami* paper, in different colors, purple, red, and yellow. So I just folded away, and each time I folded one, it flew off into the tree."

"Wait," asked Clara. "How many did you fold?"

Yuka paused and with a crook of her neck said, "I'm not quite sure. Oh my! You know there is a Japanese tradition that if you want to wish someone well, you have to fold one thousand cranes within a year and then present them to that person."

"You were in there for a year?" asked Clara.

"Well, no," said Yuka. "But it was a long time, but I didn't get tired. So I just kept folding as they flew up into the tree. They were so beautiful. And then I folded the last one and as it flew into the branch, I said, '*utsukushī*.' That's Japanese for beautiful, and then everything went dark."

"That must have been when the leaf fell!" said Clara excitedly. "Yuka, you may have folded one thousand cranes to honor the Longevity Tree!"

"I don't know," said Yuka doubtfully. "Maybe it was a thousand? But it was definitely a lot!"

Both Yuka and Clara laughed.

Yuka looked at Clara with her soulful brown eyes and asked, "Guardian Crane told me that I was healed with a liquid made of gold that the cute rabbit made for me."

"It was," said Clara. "I saw the golden leaf fall myself."

"Hmmm," murmured Yuka. "I think I know what the gold means."

Clara's ears perked up as she focused in on Yuka.

"There's a Japanese tradition called *kintsugi*," began Yuka. "When a piece of pottery is broken, the pieces are glued back together using gold. Though fixed, the cracks are still there, but the shiny gold fills in the cracks. The cracks of gold remind us what was broken, but also that it's whole again. I think the gold from the Longevity Tree fixed all my broken pieces and gave me a new life."

Clara bit her lip and reached out for Yuka's hands. They tenderly held each other's fingers, comforted by their friendship. Yuka then looked side to side cautiously as she gently pulled her hands away.

In a hushed tone, Yuka asked, "Can I tell you something?"

Clara leaned in, "Sure."

Yuka paused and then whispered, "I can feel my Qi."

Clara looked confused and asked, "What do you mean? We can all feel our Qi."

"No Clara," said Yuka as she bore her bare forearms for Clara to see. "I can feel every ounce of it and see it too."

Clara looked down and suddenly saw the faint bluish branching channels of Qi just below Yuka's skin. "Whoa!"

"The Longevity Tree fixed me, and well, I think I'm more whole than before," said Yuka.

Clara reached out with her fingertips and traced the soothing bluish channels of Qi along Yuka's forearm.

"That's amazing," said Clara. "Do you have more powers now?"

"I don't know," said Yuka. "I don't feel any different, except I feel really strong and healthy. I haven't tried to invoke anything yet, but I'm so much more connected to my Qi."

"Wow, that's incredible," said Clara as she pulled her hands back. "So what now?"

Yuka cheerily shrugged her shoulders and with a grin said, "I'm really hungry. How about some *tamago?*"

Clara and Yuka laughed.

TWENTY - SEVEN

The next morning, the Azen Warriors gathered with their guardians at the communal meal table. They had once again changed back into their clothes from home and were eating lunch.

Clara and Yuka ate lightly as they talked and giggled amongst themselves with the Guardian Panda and Crane chiming in here and there. Sung and Daniel gorged on their food, knowing that it was their last day on Azen before the next battle. But every now and then, Daniel would steal a furtive glance at Yuka, who now looked lively and cheerful. His guilt was still a weight on his heart that he didn't know how to vanquish.

"Empress and emperor warriors," said the Guardian Panda as he looked at the four warriors. "It is that time once more for you to portal your way back home."

"Do we have to go?" Clara whined playfully.

The Guardian Panda blinked his eyes a few times and responded, "You may stay, but I think you'll miss your mom's spicy wontons."

Clara laughed and sheepishly said, "You're probably right. Okay, let's go."

Everyone raised themselves out of their seats. But Clara couldn't help noticing that Yuka and Daniel had said very little to each other. As the guardians turned away from the table, she looked at her friends just as they were getting up.

"Psst," whispered Clara quietly as everyone turned to her.

Clara admired Sung's handsomeness, the boyish good looks of Daniel, and Yuka's cheeriness. She smiled as if everyone knew as they brought their fists up, elbows out and all said, "For Azen."

The warriors gathered up their weapons and ran alongside their guardians as they made the walk back up to the Portal Circle. As they approached, everyone saw that the leaders of the kingdoms were all waiting for them in the center of the Portal Circle. They were facing in the direction of their respective Portal Books. Their entourages stood behind the Portal Circle.

Clara suddenly felt she needed to straighten up as she whispered to the Guardian Panda, "What's going on?"

"Just some parting words, Empress Warrior Wu," said the Guardian Panda.

Clara nodded and along with the warriors, briskly walked to their Portal Books and faced into the circle. The guardians took up their places in front of each Portal Book.

The Ascendent, in a regal *kimono* styled robe that draped over her back, stepped out and smiled.

"Azen Warriors," exclaimed the Ascendant. "Before you depart, your kingdom leaders and I wanted to offer you our gratitude. What is expected of you has not been insignificant, but you honor us with your resilience, determination, and bravery. I know that this battle was challenging as there were unexpected circumstances."

Daniel instinctively looked down just as the Ascendant turned to look at him and Sung.

"But despite the unexpected challenges, Emperor Warriors Kim and Nguyen persevered against the Warlock army and held them at bay, buying valuable time for Empress Warrior Wu to complete her mission with the Guardian Crane and Panda, to bring back our most precious Empress Warrior Satoh. For that, we are eternally grateful. *Domo-arigato.*"

The warriors and guardians bowed toward the kingdom leaders as they bowed back solemnly.

"Empress and emperor warriors, the next time we will see you will be for the last battle, so practice well. I know we shall be victorious," said the Ascendant confidently.

The kingdom leaders then walked to their respective guardians and thanked them. Then they rotated clockwise and thanked the next warrior until the kingdom leaders each had a chance to thank each of the warriors. When they returned to their own warriors, they bowed fondly one more time. They then stepped out of the Portal Circle and walked away with their entourages.

"When is the fourth lunar eclipse?" asked Sung.

The Guardian Tiger looked up into the sky and spotted the faint moon and answered, "That would be *pāru*, the fourth moon. About three weeks your time, Emperor Warrior Kim."

"*Pāru?* Is that Japanese for pearl?" asked Yuka.

"Yes, it is, Empress Warrior Satoh," said the Guardian Crane.

"I see," responded Yuka under her breath.

"That will give me time to manifest like crazy back home," exclaimed Daniel.

"So what's everyone going to do once they get back home?" asked Clara as she began to unsling her bow and quiver. A panda attendant came up to take it.

"I think I'm going for a swim," said Daniel as he handed the Club Horn of *Kting Voar* to a buffalo attendant.

"Don't you think it's odd that the Wu fire warrior is a swimmer?" Sung quipped as he stepped out of his shoes.

"And this is coming from the original Iceman who loves spicy kimchi," Daniel responded snidely.

"Oooo…" Sung teased. "You made an Asian joke bro!"

Daniel laughed and extended his fist in Sung's direction as he blurted out, "Fire!"

Sung stood tall, extended his fist and responded, "And ice!"

Clara just slipped out of her shoes as a panda attendant took them away, "*Dò-jeh,*" she said. "Me? I think it's about dinner time for me. I hope I'm not late."

Everyone laughed and everyone looked at Yuka, who had just slipped out of her shoes and looked up.

"And how about you Yuka?" asked Clara.

"Me? Oh not much. I think it was just about dinner time too when the Portal Book took me away. I hope I'm not late too! And don't forget to manifest! Especially you guys," said Yuka.

Daniel opened his mouth but found that the words would not tumble out when Sung answered for them, "We won't. But I'll be spending more time with my *abeoji*. Oh, that's Korean for…"

"Father!" everyone said in unison to Sung's shock as he turned red.

Everyone laughed and smiled warmly at each other.

"Okay everyone," Yuka began. "I'll see you all soon. Clara and Guardian Panda, thank you for risking your lives to rescue me."

Clara and the Guardian Panda nodded graciously to Yuka as she bowed back. She then turned toward her Guardian Crane and looked up at her soulful beady eyes.

"Guardian Crane," said Yuka soulfully, as she said *Thank you for saving my life*, in Japanese, "*Watashi no inochi wo tasukute kurete arigatō.*"

Yuka bowed deeply to the Guardian Crane, who looked at Yuka with fondness and nodded as she closed her beady eyes. The grand red feathers atop her head dipped forward gracefully.

Yuka picked up her red feathery quill brush and wrote *home* in Japanese. Moments later, fiery embers spiraled out as she closed her eyes as the warm light enveloped her. Daniel stared at Yuka and in that last moment before she faded away, Daniel mouthed silently, "I'm sorry."

Daniel wiped his eye as the Guardian Buffalo asked, "Is everything okay, Emperor Warrior Nguyen?"

Daniel looked up at the stern face of the Guardian Buffalo and shook his head as he replied. "Oh, no, it was nothing. Just the bright light made me squint."

"I see," said the Guardian Buffalo. "Remember to close your eyes before you portal away."

"Yes, Guardian Buffalo," replied Daniel as he turned to Sung and Clara. "I'll see you guys soon!"

"Emperor Warrior Nguyen," said the stoic Guardian Buffalo as Daniel turned to him. "You fought valiantly. The challenge was great, and you did not turn away from it."

"Then why do I feel so awful?" asked Daniel.

"You have three weeks to figure that out. Use them wisely," advised the Guardian Buffalo.

"You know everything, don't you, Guardian Buffalo?" asked Daniel.

"Not everything," he replied. "But I do know when you may need to be reminded that you can make things right."

Daniel nodded as he said *thank you* in Vietnamese, "*cảm ơn bạn*, Guardian Buffalo. I'll see you soon."

Daniel wrote the Vietnamese word for *home*, and soon, he too vanished into the bright light.

"Have fun with your *abeoji* when you get home," said Clara playfully as she picked up her bamboo brush.

Sung laughed and saw Clara vanish in the bright light.

"Ugh!" Sung let out in frustration as the Guardian Tiger looked up and asked, "What is wrong, Emperor Warrior Kim?"

Sung looked up with a playful look as he uttered, "I'm last again. See you soon, Guardian Tiger!"

"Yes, Emperor Warrior Kim," said the Guardian Tiger as he closed his eyes as the bright light of the Portal Book appeared.

TWENTY - EIGHT

Yuka felt the warm light cocoon her entire body. As she traveled along with the light, she thought back to her tortuous experience, and she shuddered at the memory. However, being rescued by her Guardian Crane and the rest of the rescue team that risked their lives to save her warmed her heart. But thinking of Clara made her smile as she knew she had a bond with her that was deeper than friendship. It was a bond borne of Azen.

Soon, she felt a slight jolt as the warm pink light that seeped through her closed eyelids started to fade away. She let out a breath through pursed lips before her eyes fluttered open.

She quickly looked left and right from her kneeling position by the side of her bed. All was quiet, and not a soul was around. She looked down at her Portal Book and saw that the fiery Japanese character for *home* had started to fade. She placed her hands at the center of the silken bamboo pages and spread them outward until finally, the Japanese character had turned to solid black.

She looked down at her hands and she turned them upward, looking at her palms. She looked cautiously about and smiled as she pushed up her sleeves to her elbows. As she looked down at her forearms, she focused and smiled as the bluish lines of Qi glowed gently beneath her pale skin. Her eyes sparkled as she saw small bursts of white light traverse along the Qi lines. *What does it all mean,* she thought? *Why could she see her Qi? What was this gift that the Longevity Tree had given to her?* But she had no answers.

Her eyes darted upward as she heard footsteps approach. She gasped and glanced at her forearms just as the bluish lines of Qi started to fade way. She quickly rolled down her sleeves just as she caught sight of the open page of the Portal Book, which had magically created a half-finished grid of a Japanese lesson.

"Yuka?" said a voice from behind the hanging sheet partition.

Yuka straightened up just as her father appeared from behind it. He looked down at her, the wrinkles around his eyes deepening as a grin spread across his face. The crease around his mouth was clear, making him look older than he was. He had allowed his hair to begin to grow, but the ample gray was starting to show. As a fisherman, he worked a hard life to support his family of four along with his wife.

As he slipped off his worn-out black shoes and stepped into the room, Yuka looked him up and down. Despite their humbler home away from home, he was dressed in dark gray slacks, a rumpled short-sleeve dress shirt open at the top, and a white t-shirt underneath. His belt was cinched tightly as he had lost some weight.

"*Otosan*," smiled Yuka as a gut of emotion welled up within her, causing her to gulp.

"We missed you at lunch," her father said as he gingerly walked to her side of the bed with his right hand behind his back.

Yuka looked flustered and glanced down at the Portal Book once more and was comforted to see that the Japanese lesson was still there. She looked back up at her father and answered, "Oh, I must have lost track of time. I was practicing."

"Oh?" her father responded. "Your mother did not see you here about forty-five minutes ago when she came looking for you."

Yuka quickly realizing how much time she had been away. She let out, "Oh, I stepped out for a moment. She must have missed me."

"Must have been," said her father when he reassuringly said, "Well, no worries. I brought you something."

Her father pulled out from behind his back a plate covered in a white napkin. As he placed it on the bed beside Yuka, he pulled off the napkin.

"*Tamago!*" said Yuka.

"And SPAM," said her father with a chuckle.

Yuka looked up at her father and simply said in Japanese for *thank you* as she nodded, "*Domo arigato.*"

Her father smiled and said, "It's what the women wanted to cook today as a shipment of fresh eggs arrived this morning."

Yuka couldn't help but lick her lips as she pulled the plate toward her and looked at the glistening *tamago* along with the three slices of SPAM. *Definitely a Japanese American meal*, she thought.

"Still practicing your Japanese?" asked her father as he admired his daughter's beautiful calligraphy.

With a grin, Yuka said, "I am."

"It's really beautiful," said her father approvingly.

"Thanks," said Yuka appreciatively when she uttered softly, "*Papa?*"

"Yes?"

"You're not going to go away again, right?" she asked.

Her father looked at her then looked into his lap before saying, "No, I won't. I'm home now."

"Was it hard for you being away from us?" asked Yuka as she turned toward her father.

Her father nodded his head and muttered, "It was torture being away from all of you. I wasn't sure if I could return, but I'm home now."

Yuka felt her heart skip a beat when she pressed her father, "How can you be sure?"

Her father let out another sigh, glanced down at Yuka before peering out through the window. He took in the sunny blue sky and simply said, "A bird told me."

Yuka's eyes lit up as she let out, "A bird?"

Her father chuckled and looked dotingly at Yuka. "Well not any bird, a big pelican!"

Yuka laughed as her father went on. "Remember those big pelicans along the dock?"

Yuka nodded enthusiastically before she remarked, "But dad, we're in Arizona."

The chuckle from her father was disarming as he let out a sigh. "I saw the pelican in my dream."

"I see," said Yuka. "I kind of have a bird too."

"You do? What kind of bird?" asked her father.

With a big smile, Yuka said, "A big red-crown crane!"

Her father let out a warm laugh before he challenged his daughter, "But Yuka, we're in Arizona. The red-crown crane is only in Japan!"

Yuka let out a laugh when she said, "I saw her in my dream too!"

"I see," said her father. "So she's like your guardian animal? A guardian crane?"

Yuka froze. Her heart stopped for a moment when her father said, "guardian crane," but there was no way he could have known about her. With a stupefied look, all she could do was nod.

Her father nodded his head and looked down at the plate of *tamago* and SPAM and said, "Hurry up and eat, Yuka."

Yuka pulled the plate toward her as her father slipped out a pair of chopsticks wrapped in a napkin from his pocket.

As she took the chopsticks, Yuka looked up and said, "I'm glad you're back."

"Me too," her father said lovingly.

TWENTY - NINE

The Warlock lumbered heavily into the examination room, each of his steps reverberating on the stone floor. The Harvester tree and a howling demon tree spun around from the back counter.

"My Lord," uttered the Harvester as he and his assistant bowed.

The Warlock ignored them as his yellowish eyes fixed onto the stone examination table. It was bare, but he looked down on it with consternation as he raised his two massive fists and pounded the table, cracking it open along its width. He heaved his two fists into the air and brought them down onto the cracked stone table once more, sending the two halves splintering apart onto the floor.

The two trees stepped backwards as their top branches recoiled into their trunk at the Warlock's colossal might.

The Warlock leveled his gaze on the Harvester tree and ordered, "Next time! No more of these games, we will just cut it out!"

Their shriveled branches fluttered nervously in fright as both howling demon trees nodded.

The Warlock let out a heavy breath, spun around and stomped out of the room. His heavy footsteps alerted his Demon Lords in the throne room of his approach. As he hurried to the throne room, he could see his fearful Demon Lords scurry out of the throne room and into the primary wing.

He entered his expansive throne room and looked up at the newly installed slab of glass in the roof. He marched in a huff, walked up the three stone slab steps, and seated himself on the cold throne. He pushed himself into the back of the throne and his eyes stared at the orb. He picked it up gingerly and stared into its glassy darkness as swirls of green glided by. But when the new white swirl glided by, he smiled and uttered, "You may have escaped, but not all was lost."

THANK YOU

If you have come to the end of "Clara Wu and the Rescue," which is Book Three of the Clara Wu Books, I hope you enjoyed the harrowing rescue that was depicted in this story. I also hope you enjoyed seeing more of panda and crane life in this story to spark your curious imagination as to how big and expansive the world of Azen is.

I also hope that you could identify with one or more of the characters. And let's not forget the Guardian Panda, White Tiger, Red Crown Crane and the Water Buffalo.

My goal is to create authentic and fun Asian American stories so that Asian American readers can see themselves as the heroes. We've always been, we just need more writers to put them on paper.

Please tell your friends about this book series and flip to the section where I give some tips on how to promote this book to better Asian Representation!

A big thank you to my new illustrator, SantiSann who brought my characters to life with incredible talent. Check out SantiSann's work at:

Instagram: @santisann88

Another thank you goes out to Gloria Tsai for voicing the audio teaser for Book One which you may find on YouTube by searching for "Clara Wu." Check out her work at:

http://www.gloriatsai.com/voiceover.html

I also wanted to take a moment to thank my editor, Felicia Lee of Cambridge Editors, who has been my editor since my first book. Check out her profile at:

https://cambridgeeditors.com/editors/

Please be sure to check out **www.clarawubooks.com** and **www.vincentsstories.com** where you can check out my two other books, which are also available on Amazon:

The Purple Heart

The Tamago Stories

There are two more books in this exciting young adult Asian American fantasy series and the next one will be coming out soon! Flip to the next page to see the title of book four!

C2E3

"Clara Wu and the Portal Book," Book One of the Clara Wu Books, is now an Award-Winning Book! In the Fall of 2022, Clara Wu and her Guardian Panda showed fantasy fans that stories about Asian American heroes and their cultural animals can enrich the fantasy genre!

Book Four

Clara Wu

AND THE

Final Battle

by Vincent Yee

Available Now!

ABOUT THE AUTHOR

Vincent Yee was born in Boston, Massachusetts. For most of his career, he has worked for several Fortune 100 companies in various managerial roles. At all other times, he has a vision…

"To write for better Asian Representation."

In 2022, he became an award-winning author for the first book in his YA-Fantasy series, "Clara Wu and the Portal Book," that placed second in the overall YA-Fantasy category at The BookFest. The remaining books of the "Clara Wu and the World of Azen," were all published in one year and they were: The Jade Labyrinth, Rescue, Final Battle and Warlock.

He has two other books prior and his first novel, "The Purple Heart," is a story about love and courage set during the Japanese American experience in WWII. His second book is a collection of 8 riveting contemporary Asian American short stories.

Vincent Yee was a former National President for the National Association of Asian American Professionals (NAAAP). He also co-founded the ERG at his last employer and led it with an amazing team, to be one of the largest ERGs with over 450+ members within a few months. He's also been known to create artistic culinary dishes for friends. When he is not writing, he may be binging a K-Drama on Netflix. He now lives in Cambridge, Massachusetts.

HOW TO SUPPORT

www.clarawubooks.com

Nothing makes a book popular and successful without its fans so please spread the word!

1) **FACEBOOK**
   Go to facebook.com/clarawubooks and **LIKE** the page.
2) **INSTAGRAM and TIK TOK**
   Go to Instagram and Tik Tok and like @clarawubooks
3) **SELFIE or PICTURE**
   TAKE a selfie/picture with yourself or your young reader that you are comfortable with, along with the book, and post to your social media and use the tags below.

   For Facebook and IG/Tik Tok tag @clarawubooks and use the hashtags #clarawubooks #AsianRepresentation #AsianStories #asianbookstagrammer

4) **WEB**
   Go to www.clarawubooks.com to find out the fun ways on how to engage with these books. You'll find my contact info there.
5) **AMAZON/GOODREADS**
   Please write a review for each book in the Clara Wu Books that you have read on Amazon or Goodreads.

6) **ASIAN SCHOOL**
   Spread the word at your child's weekend Asian programs (e.g. Chinese, Korean, Japanese, Vietnamese, etc), or martial arts/music/dance schools.

7) If you belong to a book club, please consider recommending this book for your next read. I will attend your book club over Zoom if so desired.

8) **EDUCATORS**
   Are you an elementary or high school teacher? This would be great for your students!

9) **LIBRARIES/BOOKSTORES**
   Talk to your library about adding this series to their collection. Over ten libraries in the greater Boston area now carry it.

10) **COMMUNITY ORGANATION/ERG**
    If you are part of any Asian American community organization or ERG/BRG/Affinity group, I'd be more than happy to be a speaker. Go to www.clarawubooks.com for more info.

11) If you know of any Asian American Influencers/Podcasters, please consider recommending this book to them.

12) If you would like to host a Meet the Author event over Zoom for your group of friends, your organization or your work AA group, I'll be there!

13) Lastly, you can **"Read It, Wear It!"** Flip to the next page to see the exciting **MERCH** items for Clara Wu and the World of Azen.

Let's **PROVE** that there is a market for positive and authentic Asian American stories especially ones that will give the next generation of Asian American readers, heroes that look like them.

clarawubooks.myshopify.com

Wear exciting merchandise featuring your favorite characters from the Clara Wu Books! Choose from over 100 items! Show your friends what an amazing fantasy story they've been missing! Another great way to spread the word!

DICTIONARY

Word	Language	Meaning	First Appeared In
abeoji	Korean	father	B1
aigo	Korean	oh my goodness – usually used to express annoyance or surprise	B3
Aki	Japanese	Name for a boy that means, bright and clear	B3
Annyeonghaseyo	Korean	Hello	B2
Ao Dai	Vietnamese	A traditional Vietnamese dress that is a long gown worn with trousers.	B1
appa	Kokrean	Father informal, affectionate	B2
baba	Cantonese – Chinese	Father informal, affectionate	B1
bakemono	Japanese	A shape shifter that usually comes in the form of a beautiful woman to seduce unsuspecting men	B2
ban chans	Korean	A collection of side dishes like kimchi, radish or cucumber usually served along with meals.	B1
bánh mì	Vietnamese	A Vietnamese sandwich which may contain marinaded meat and fresh picked vegetables served in a soft baguette	B2
baos	Chinese	A Chinese white bun filled a variety of ingredients.	B1
boba	Chinese	A refreshing milk tea drink with tapioca pearls	B3
budi	Korean	Please	B2
Buổi sáng tốt lành	Vietnamese	Good morning	B3

Bukdaemun	Korean	North Big Gate – One of the eight gates in Korea.	B1
cảm ơn bạn	Vietnamese	thank you	B1
char-siu wonton mein	Cantonese	Roasted pork and wonton egg noodle dish	B3
chigae	Korean	Korean stew made from a variety of ingredients.	B1
chu	Cantonese	pillar	B2
dahm	Korean	wall	B1
dali	Korean	bridge	B1
đẩy	Vietnamese	thrust	B1
dōitashimashit	Japanese	You're welcome	B3
dojang	Korean	Tae Kwan Do training hall	B3
dò-jeh	Cantonese – Chinese	thank you	B1
domo arigato	Japanese	Thank you very much	B1
dōmu		dome	B3
Dongdaemun	Korean	East Big Gate – One of the eight gates in Korea.	B1
eomma	Korean	Mother informal, affectionate	B1
fai-dee	Cantonese	Quickly or Hurry up	B3
galbi	Korean	grilled ribs (aka kalbi)	B1
gam-sa-ham-ni-da	Korean	thank you	B1
Ganbatte!	Japanese	Good luck to you!	B3
gimbap	Korean	A roll of rice and cooked items wrapped in seaweed	B2
gō	Japanese	Multi-tiered slender towers in Japan with a spire on top	B1
go	Japanese	**game played with black and white stones**	B3
gỏi cuốn	Vietnamese	Spring rolls wrapped with rice paper	B3
gong gyuck	Korean	attack	B1

gook	Korean/Mandarin	Country in its respective language however, it is taken out of context in America that has become a slur	B1
gumiho	Korean	A version of the 9 tailed fox creature that is common in east Asian culture (aka kumiho)	B2
Hạ Long Bay	Vietnamese	Famous beautiful bay in Vietnam that is also a UNESCO World Heritage Site	B1
Hangul	Korean	Writing system of the Korean language.	B1
Hirami	Japanese	Name for a girl that means, good flower	B3
Huli jing	Chinese	A version of the 9 tailed fox creature that is common in east Asian culture	B2
Huo Dou	Chinese	A large black dog that can emit flames from its mouth.	B1
Ikuchi	Japanese	Mythical sea serpents	B3
jinju	Korean	pearl	B1
jo sun	Cantonese – Chinese	Good morning in Cantonese	B1
joh-eun achim	Korean	Good morning with beautiful sun	B1
Jook	Cantonese	Similar to rice porridge served with slices of meat, preserved duck egg along with Chinese fried dough	B2
jōshō suru	Japanese	ascend	B1
jum-doong	Cantonese	tremor	B3
kabe	Japanese	wall	B1
Kalbi	Korean	grilled ribs (aka galbi)	B2
Karate	Japanese	A Japanese martial art that means *empty hand*.	B1
kata	Japanese	In Karate, a set pattern of movements that is practiced as part of training.	B1

katana	Japanese	Usually refers to a long single edged sword usually used by the Samurai.	B1
kimchi	Korean	A spicy fermented cabbage that is a delicacy in Korea.	B1
kimono	Japanese	A beautiful and traditionally wrapped garment for Japanese women that may come in a variety of colors and patterns.	B1
Kintsugi	Japanese	Art of fixing broken pottery with gold	B3
Koko wa doko	Japanese	Where am I?	B3
Konbanwa	Japanese	Good evening	B2
Kting voar	Vietnamese	Mystical horned creature that existed in Vietnam and Cambodia. Its true origin has never been determined though its unusual horns have left researchers puzzled about the creature.	B1
Kung Fu	Chinese	A Chinese martial art with many styles.	B1
makimono	Japanese	A Japanese roll of seaweed and sushi rice that may contain vegetables, fish or both.	B1
mẹ	Vietnamese	mother	B1
Michi	Japanese	Name for a girl that means, pathway	B3
Min'na doko ni iru no	Japanese	Where is everyone?	B3
moushi wake arimasen deshita	Japanese	No excuses can justify my actions and I apologize	B1
Namdaemun	Korean	South Big Gate – One of the eight gates in Korea.	B1
ngọc trai	Vietnamese	pearl	B1

nigiri	Japanese	Usually, a ball of sushi rice that is topped off with raw fish or other seafood.	B1
nue	Chinese	A creature with the face of a monkey, a body of a tiger and a venomous snake as its tail	B2
nun	Korean	snow	B3
ohayo gozaimasu	Japanese	good morning	B1
oni	Japanese	Ogre like creature that exists in Japanese folklore	B2
origami	Japanese	The art of folding paper.	B1
otosan	Japanese	father formal	B1
p̃aru	Japanese	pearl	B1
pho	Vietnamese	A Vietnamese soup noodle dish usually made from a slow cooked beef bone broth, with rice noodles and beef slices or brisket.	B1
Seodaemun	Korean	West Big Gate – One of the eight gates in Korea.	B1
seoping	Korean	surf	B1
Seosomun	Korean	West Small Gate - – One of the eight gates in Korea.	B1
shuriken	Japanese	Throwing star made popular in the era of Ninjas.	B1
shí	Mandarin	ten	B3
shí-liù	Mandarin	sixteen	B3
Sho	Japanese	Name for a boy that means, one to soar to great heights	B1
Sonomama de ite	Japanese	Remain true	

Soohorang	Korean	Tiger of Protection – *Soohoo* means protection and *rang* comes from Ho-rang-i for tiger. Known to be a sacred guardian animal in Korea.	B1
Soyōnara	Japanese	goodbye	B3
Sungeuni mangeukhaeumnida	Korean	Your grace is immeasurable	B1
surujins	Japanese	a length of rope that was weighted at both ends	B3
Tae Kwan Do	Korean	A Korean martial art that is known for its powerful and dynamic kicks.	B1
taegeuk	Korean	In Tae Kwan Do, a set pattern of movements that is practiced as part of training.	B1
Takeshi	Japanese	Name for a boy that means, a warrior	B1
tamago	Japanese	Elegant Japanese version of an egg omelette	B2
Tanchō	Japanese	cranes	B3
Tanchō! Washi	Japanese	red crown crane	B3
tatami	Japanese	A type of traditional Japanese flooring.	B1
tei hum	Cantonese – Chinese	sinkhole	B1
teng-bing	Cantonese – Chinese	wall	B1
the-oung	Vietnamese	wall	B1
thit bo voi bo	Vietnamese	well known beef dish	B1
tō	Japanese	Japanese pagoda like tower structure.	B1
tsukkome	Japanese	dive (into air)	B3
tobu	Japanese	fly	B1
toppū	Japanese	gust	B3
utsukushī	Japanese	beautiful	B3
Vovinam	Vietnamese	A Vietnamese martial art	B1
Wakaranai	Japanese	I don't understand	B3

Watashi no inochi wo tasukute kurete arigatō	Japanese	Thank you for saving my life	B3
Watashi wa kowarete imasu ka?	Japanese	I'm broken inside	B3
Watashi wa shinde imasu ka	Japanese	Am I dead?	B3
Wuxia	Mandarin	A style of Chinese movies depicting Chinese martial arts in ancient China with superhuman strength	B3
yaki onigiri	Japanese	Lightly fried rice ball with seaweed on the outside	B3
yakitori	Japanese	skewered grilled meat	B1
yi ge jiu cai san xian jiao zi	Mandarin	One leek and bamboo dumpling	B2
yi ge bai cai san xian jiao zi	Mandarin	One cabbage and bamboo dumpling	B2
yi ge san xian jiao zi	Mandarin	One pea, carrot and bamboo dumpling	B2
Yonggirang	Korean	Tiger of Courage – *Yong-gi* for courage and *rang* comes from Ho-rang-i for tiger. The Guardian Animal from the White Tiger Kingdom.	B1
Xuong Cuong	Vietnamese	howling demon trees	B3
zao shang hao	Mandarin – Chinese	good morning in Mandarin	B1
zhēnzhū	Mandarin – Chinese	pearl	B1